Paul Mannering is an award-winning writer of speculative fiction, comedy, horror and military action novels, short stories, radio plays and the occasional government report.

He lives in Wellington, New Zealand with his wife Damaris, and their two cats. Paul harbours a deep suspicion about asparagus and firmly believes we should all make an effort to be more courteous to cheese.

THE DRAKEFORTH SERIES
PUBLISHED BY IFWG

Engines of Empathy (Book 1)
Pisce of Fate (Book 2)
Time of Breath (Book 3 - released Nov 2018)

THE DRAKEFORTH SERIES BOOK 2

Pisces of

Fate

BY PAUL MANNERING

INCLUDING A BONUS,
DRAKEFORTH—RELATED SHORT STORY,
UNCERTAINTY OF GOATS

Pisces of Fate
Uncertainty of Goats (short story)

All Rights Reserved

ISBN-13: 978-1-925496-89-5

Copyright ©2018 Paul Mannering

V1.1

Pisces of Fate/Uncertainty of Goats first published separately in 2016.

Printed in Palatino Linotype and Voodoo Eye Title

IFWG Publishing International
Melbourne

www.ifwgpublishing.com

ACKNOWLEDGEMENTS

It takes a village to raise an idiot, so to all my villagers, thank you. Thanks go to: Damaris, for being the love of my life and a most patient writing widow. To my family, my love and appreciation for your support. To my beta readers, I applaud your literary constitution for getting through those early drafts. Thanks to Ash and Danielle, for being the best kids a dad could ever want. And my humble gratitude to the readers. I encourage you to breed. Your literary genes need to be passed on to successive generations.

This one is for Dad, my favourite marine biologist.

TABLE OF CONTENTS

CHAPTER 1

In the warm tropical waters of the Aardvark Archipelago swims a fish that no one likes. The consensus is that the species, Deiectio Piscis, colloquially known as the "Poo Fish", is a bit of a jerk. Inedible to humans and other predators, the Diarrhoea Fish has evolved explosive bowel evacuations as a defensive mechanism when threatened.

Ascott Pudding stopped typing and looked up, staring out from under the palm-leaf roof of his beach hut veranda. He gazed over the sunlit crystal waters of the lagoon, past the jagged fangs of the coral reef where the waves burst into foam, all the way to the horizon, where he saw the pale smudge of a man striding across the low waves.

"This," he announced to the parrot that was drawing with crayons and paper on the table, "may require pants."

"Bithcuith," the parrot replied around the stub of *Hibiscus Yellow* clamped in its beak.

By the time Ascott had dressed in shorts and a loose shirt, and walked to the end of the small island's narrow dock, the man was crossing the lagoon. Even at low tide, the water was two metres deep. As far as Ascott could tell, the man wasn't walking on stilts, or wearing some kind of boat shoes. He was barefoot and walking across the pristine surface of the sea with the same casual stride of someone crossing a well-tended lawn.

"Morning!" Ascott called. The man raised a hand and shaded his eyes. From the dock, Ascott could see the walker was wearing the first pair of trousers he had seen in nearly two years. The man also wore a loose white shirt, a white hat and dark sunglasses. A pair of white sneakers hung around his neck by their laces and he clutched the handle of a small suitcase in his hand.

"Ascott Pudding?" the man said, looking up as he reached the water below the dock.

"Yes?"

"Son of Daedius and Krismiss, also known as Dorothy, Pudding?"

"The very same." Ascott stepped back as the man climbed on to the dock and set his suitcase down.

"And you are?" Ascott said as the slender man removed his sunglasses.

"You have a sister named Charlotte?" the man asked, ignoring the earlier question.

"I have a sister named Charlotte, yes. Look, what is this all—? AARRGH!" Ascott fell back on the dock, blood streaming from his nose.

The man put his sunglasses back on and said, "I've travelled a long way to punch a member of the Pudding family in the face. Now that chore is over, how about a cup of tea, hmm?" He picked up his suitcase and walked away towards the small house above the beach.

T he tea tasted of blood, which Ascott assumed was because he couldn't smell anything through his bruised nose. He pressed a damp cloth against his face and regarded the man sitting across from him. The stranger had introduced himself as Vole Drakeforth and, when he wasn't punching strangers in the face, he looked almost civilised, like a crocodile in a business suit. Inside the clothes he seemed tall and thin, with dark hair and skin that looked as manicured as his nails. His eyes were a piercing blue and he wore an expression of mild contempt that seemed habitual.

"So...you're a god?" Ascott said eventually.

"I'm a retired god. I'm Arthur, the founder of Arthurianism."

"I thought you said your name was Vole Drakeforth?"

"It is Vole Drakeforth. I also happen to be Arthur."

"Aren't you supposed to have a beard or something?"

"The problem with religion," Drakeforth said, "is that everything becomes codified."

"Which is why you don't have a beard?"

"Which is why I'm retired."

"You've retired to a small island in the Aardvark Archipelago?" Ascott blinked. The island was small enough without sharing it with anyone else.

"No, this is just a place I wanted to visit, specifically to punch you in the face."

"Oh, right." Ascott dabbed his tender nose. "It hardly seems fair to punch me in the nose because you're angry with an ancestor of mine."

"Well, I am having an entirely different encounter with your sister," Drakeforth explained.

"Please, don't try to explain the quantum nature of perception to me again. It makes my head ache worse than my nose."

Drakeforth ignored the request. "Simply put, at a quantum level, everything is taking place at the same time. While I am here, drinking tea with you, I am also drinking tea with your sister, Charlotte."

Ascott groaned and sipped the blood-flavoured tea.

Drakeforth watched Charlotte's younger brother wince. There was a definite family resemblance. They both had hair that black-brown shade of the possibly still edible bits of burnt toast. He decided to delay the bad news for a moment longer.

"What do you actually do here?" Drakeforth said, looking around at the bamboo-walled hut.

"I sleep with fish," Ascott said.

"Why?"

"Pardon?"

Drakeforth spoke with exaggerated slowness. "Why do you sleep with fish?"

"Because to truly know a fish, you have to interact with them completely. Swim where they swim, eat what they eat, sleep when they sleep. The more we know about the natural world around us, the more we can know about ourselves and our place in the Universe."

"What if I told you that fish exist only to make more fish. The only reason they are so dedicated to making more fish is that bigger fish eat them all the time. There's your parallel to humanity's place in the natural order of things right there," Drakeforth said.

"I've seen species do things that no one has ever observed before. I've learned about their mating habits, their life cycles, the way they protect themselves from predators. I'm sure that they know more than they're letting on."

Drakeforth stared at the thin, slightly unkempt young man who had Charlotte Pudding's eyes and a swollen nose. "Have you told anyone else about these ideas of yours?"

"Not yet. I'm writing a book on it. A study of the fish species of the Aardvark Archipelago."

"Good for you. I suppose you survive on a diet of fresh fish and milknuts?"

Ascott blushed slightly. "I don't eat that much fish. There's a girl, Shoal, who comes from Montaban every couple of weeks with frozen pizzas."

The parrot flew up and landed on the table, where it tested the strength of one of the tea mugs by biting it.

"Get off the table, Tacus." Ascott waved his hand ineffectually at the bird.

"Bithcuith," the parrot said.

"Your bird appears to have a speech impediment," Drakeforth observed.

"Nobody'th perfect!"

"Tacus, this is Vole Drakeforth. Say hello to the nice man."

Tacus hopped from foot to foot and kept his beak shut.

"He is an excellent judge of character," Drakeforth said.

"Are you hungry? I can heat up a pizza?"

"Bithcuith!" Tacus squawked.

"Not necessary; the tea is quite sufficient," Drakeforth said.

"I really did see you walking across the ocean?"

"Hardly," Drakeforth said with a snort. "I flew into Montaban, then I got directions from some fishermen, then I hired a small boat, which—"

"I'm sure I saw you walking on water," Ascott said.

"—Which sank. From there I walked."

"From Montaban? That's twenty miles."

"From some point between here and Montaban, it was far less than twenty miles."

"That's still quite an achievement," Ascott said.

"It is possible that instead of walking I could have simply materialised on your doorstep and punched you in the face. However, doing that would have been far too easy and it's nice to appreciate something that you have actually worked for. Besides, it was a nice day for a stroll."

"Now that you bring it up," Ascott said thickly. "This may be a silly question, with an obvious answer, but why in the Hibiscus did you come all this way to punch me in the face?"

"You've been here since your parents died?" Drakeforth asked.

"Pretty much. I ran away after their funeral."

"Leaving Charlotte to take care of things?" Drakeforth made the accusation sound like a throwaway remark.

"She is good at taking care of things."

"Yes – if the manuscript she hasn't written yet is to be believed, she will soon be taking care of your great-grandfather."

"What?"

"You haven't been paying attention." Drakeforth nodded.

"I have, but mostly to the fish," Ascott said.

"Your sister, Charlotte, is dying. She is also presently uncovering a grave conspiracy to enslave the world and discovering the truth about many things, including the true source of empathic energy."

Ascott's mind reeled with cold shock. "Charlotte always has been good at multi-tasking," he managed.

"So I am seeing," Drakeforth agreed.

"Charlotte…is dying? I need to go home." Ascott stood up and turned in a complete circle while trying to decide what to do next. He didn't have anything to pack other than the elderly typewriter and hundreds of pages of notes, drawings and manu-script.

When he turned back around, Drakeforth was gone.

"Bithcuith!" Tacus squawked.

CHAPTER 2

The clear waters of the Aardvark Archipelago were as warm as a bath just before it gets too cold to be comfortable and you start thinking about actually having to get out. Ascott floated on his face, breathing through a snorkel and peering down at the coral fish through large goggles. He had left his canoe anchored on the outer edge of the reef and for the last few hours had been following a bright red male *zyngus* as it swam from seaweed frond to seaweed frond. The zyngus was dining on the tiny *aphish* molluscs that swarmed over the dark green sea plants that waved in the current.

Ascott came out here to think, to work through things in his own way. Crowds, noise, and the insufferable input of the world left him feeling nauseous. Floating in the warm brine of the ocean, he could hear only his steady breathing, and review the ticker tape of his thoughts in peace.

Charlotte was dying. Not like Mum and Dad, there for breakfast one morning and gone by lunchtime. This was the slow unravelling of a life. Like a sand sculpture eroding under the waves of the rising tide.

Charlotte was dying.

Ascott mentally walked around the idea, writing it on his mind's Thinking Wall and pacing around it, considering what it meant. Charlotte dead. Dead as Mum and Dad. Dead as everyone else in the Pudding family line. Being an orphaned adult was bad enough. However, the thought of losing his entire family, Ascott felt, left an emptiness that could not be filled.

The zyngus flicked the feathery fronds of its tail and zipped downwards to a fresh buffet of molluscs. Ascott waved his arms in the water, propelling himself forward and maintaining his observation.

He hadn't cried when his parents died. The news came via an email from Charlotte, sent to him at Brix University where he was in his first year of studying marine biology. That moment was an anchor stone in his life. The lecturer had been speaking on the diversity of sea life in the Aardvark Archipelago. The potential for unknown species and behaviours to be observed, catalogued and presented to the world was breath-taking, he enthused.

The email said,

Scotty,
Mum and Dad are dead.
I'm making the arrangements.
Please call.
Love C.
PS: I'm calling dibs on the old desk.

Ascott had stood up in the lecture hall, the air having left his lungs and the room in a sudden rush of shock. His vision blurring, he stumbled over a haze of brightly coloured legs and shoes. He had just reached the aisle when a voice crashed in on him.

"Pudding?" the lecturer's voice cut through the kaleidoscope fog. "What are you doing?"

"I...have to go," Ascott managed.

"Where is so important that you go at once?"

"There...I have to go *there*." Ascott had waved a tremulous hand at the projected image at the island of Montaban, the only permanently inhabited island in the archipelago.

With the vacuum around him growing, Ascott blundered out of the hall. He had collapsed on a bench outside in the quad, gasping for air and feeling the sweat turn to ice water on his skin.

He took a sharp breath now, feeling the almost mechanical whisper of the air in the snorkel tube. Moving his arms, he felt the tension drain away again. Slow, deep breaths allowed the anxiety to fade.

Charlotte. He'd barely spoken to her since their parents' funeral. Ascott remembered staring, puzzled, at the people who claimed to have known his Mum and Dad and now mourned their passing in a way Ascott could not.

Ascott's sister had graduated college the year before their parents died. She had studied computer psychology and empathic systems programming, and was working in the field when it happened. She related to people in a way that Ascott never could, so it was better for her to deal with the stream of grieving faces. Charlotte knew what to say and how to accept the heartfelt condolences of the mourners.

Ascott had walked out of their parents' house smothered by the same sense of asphyxiation that had hit him when he received his sister's email. Charlotte had found him in the garden, pale, shaking, and short of breath.

"You okay, Scotty?" she said in the almost formal way of siblings with nothing in common.

"Yeah, just stuffy in there. I have to go." He couldn't look her in the eye.

"Back to Brix? It's a bit soon isn't it?"

"No, the Aardvark Archipelago." He waved vaguely southward.

"Why do you want to go there?" Charlotte sounded more like their mother than ever.

"Fish. I need to swim with the fish."

"There's Dad's aquarium, you could stick your head in that if you think it will help."

"Goodbye, Charlotte. Thanks for taking care of everything."

Ascott had gone straight from the house to the airport. He had found a zippilin flight that would (eventually) reach Montaban. That it wasn't a top tourist destination had reassured his need for isolation.

The zyngus vanished into a thick mat of weed called *Bloody Seaweed* by the local people. The name came from the strong, sinewy nature of the strands, which made clearing snarls of it from outboard motor propellers a frustrating and time-consuming chore. The motors, like most technology in Montaban, ran on imported empathic batteries. They also used solar panels to take advantage of the giga-wams of free energy pouring out of the sky on a daily basis.

Ascott took a deep breath through the snorkel tube and dived down. The warm water slid past, cocooning him. Underwater he could fly, moving his arms and legs in gentle beats as he soared and plummeted. A single tanned fish in a Universe of other colours.

The Zyngus fish, Ascott mentally dictated, feeds on the tiny Aphish molluscs that swarm the broad leaves of seaweed in the sheltered lagoons and reefs of the Aardvark Archipelago. Using its specially adapted snout, the zyngus sucks up the shellfish whole and it is either a testament to the aphish's sense of fatalism or an indication of their complete lack of perception that they do not seem at all concerned by this decimation of their numbers. It is yet to be determined if they view the zyngus fish with a sense of religious awe, or if, as the data suggests, they are less aware of this predator's involvement in their life cycle than the seaweed is of the aphish that live on its fronds.

The sudden awareness that he was in desperate need of air disrupted this train of thought. Ascott swam upwards through an exhaled stream of silver bubbles. Breaking the surface, he drew breath through the curved tube of his snorkel and resumed floating and observing the underwater landscape.

With no sign of the zyngus, Ascott swam out from the reef and explored new territory. In the last year and a half, he had identified and named one hundred and thirty-six new species of sea life. Each one received an entry in his *Encyclopaedia Brixichthyus*.

The bottom dropped away here in a long, steady decline to the deeper ocean. Ascott knew that the islands were a mountain range, with the summits broaching the surface of the water, and the slopes spreading gently out towards a distant submarine plain.

The seaweed changed out here, becoming thicker and more gnarled, like old-growth forest. It obscured his view of any fish that might be down there. With one last intake of breath, Ascott swam down. The water pressed in on all sides as he kicked his way through the thermoclines. Reaching the bottom, he crouched in a patch of cold sand and waited.

Without SCRAM (Self-Contained Reticulating Air Mechanism) gear, he could hold his breath for about three minutes. The water at this depth was still clear, though several degrees cooler than the layers above. Around him were rocky outcrops, covered in seaweed, coral and shells. The fish he saw bustling about were familiar to him and not worthy of closer observation.

When the fire in his lungs became unbearable, Ascott pushed himself upwards. With a few quick strokes, he rose towards the light, sparks popping behind his eyes and waste air bubbling out of his snorkel. Breaking the surface, he puffed the last of the water out of the tube and took a deep breath. A pair of bare feet, sticking out of the bottom of a pair of white linen trousers, stood level with his eyes.

Ascott spat the snorkel out of his mouth and peered upwards, shading his eyes against the bright sunlight.

Drakeforth stood on the water, the sun silhouetting him in a dazzling halo as he regarded Ascott, mostly submerged at his feet.

"It's quite good," Drakeforth declared. "And I don't say that about anything."

"What?" Ascott asked, referring to both the vision before him and the cryptic statement.

"Your book. The *Encyclopaedia of Fish*. I don't imagine anyone will read it. At least not outside of a few zealous fish-fanciers and some half-senile academics. But kudos to you for giving it a go."

"It's not finished," Ascott said, unsure whether to be offended or just ignore everything after the initial compliment.

"The problem with life's works is that they take a lifetime to complete. The number of people who don't know when to stop is ridiculous. Aspen, Guaco, Califralli, Meditch—all of them devoted their lives to creating the seminal work on their chosen subject and all died within a month of writing *The End* for the first time."

A strange sense of vertigo spun Ascott's senses like a gyrotop.

"I don't quite understand your point," he said.

"Exactly." Drakeforth nodded and sank into a crouch, the light waves barely sweeping over his feet. "There's too much effort put into things that do not matter." He extended a hand. Ascott took it, unsure what the gesture meant. Drakeforth stood up, pulling Ascott out of the water like a small child. His sense of unbalance grew as he found himself standing on the surface of the ocean.

"You're saying that I should stop writing the encyclopaedia?" Ascott asked.

"Not at all. I'm saying you should stop making it the sum total of your existence. You came here to escape the world. Isn't that enough? You don't need to justify your hermitage by producing anything. Certainly not something that very few people are ever going to give a monkey's mandible about."

Ascott frowned. "I like fish."

"I like cheese, but you don't see me devoting my life to writing a pseudo-academic thesis describing every variety of coagulated curd from *Albis* to *Zoostra*." Drakeforth's gaze went to the horizon, where a tiny black dot was approaching. "You," he said, putting an arm awkwardly around Ascott's shoulder, "need a hobby."

A scott sat up with a start. He blinked the salt water from his eyes and looked about. The dugout canoe he used for travelling to his dive spots rocked underneath him. The sea and sky, in their contrasting shades of blue, were calm and still. He frowned at a buzzing sound. A black dot on the horizon buzzed like an angry bee, bearing down on him. Drakeforth had vanished again.

The approaching shape resolved itself into a long, flat-bottomed wave boat with an oversized outboard motor mounted on the back. Shoal, daughter of Sandy and Palm Smith, liked to drive with the throttle wide open and the spray pluming out the back. The narrow boat skidded sideways across the waves and Shoal cut the engine. The two craft bobbed and bumped together in the same way Vector's Pygmy Whales do when they initiate courtship.

"What are you doing way out here?" Shoal asked.

She was close to Ascott's age. More at home on water than land, Shoal kept her sun-bleached hair cropped short, which just made her piercing blue eyes seem even larger. Lithe and deeply tanned, she had the casual approach to clothing of most Montabanians, who believed it should be practical and easy to swim in.

"Research," Ascott replied, blushing harder under his tan.

"Fish," Shoal said dismissively. "I've always been more interested in eating them than watching them."

"I eat fish," Ascott said.

"No, you don't. If I didn't deliver these pizzas to you every couple of weeks, you'd starve to death."

Ascott shrugged. What Shoal lacked in common tact, she made up for in blunt honesty.

"Anchovies don't count," she added, lifting a large chiller box out of the bottom of her boat. Ascott stood up, the canoe rocking underneath him, his knees automatically bending slightly as he moved with the sway. "Thanks," he said, taking the box of frozen pizzas.

"Did that fella find you?" Shoal said, her hands resting on her hips as she stood in her boat, swaying with the gentle motion of the swell.

"White suit and hat?" Ascott replied. "Yeah, he showed up."

"I wondered what happened to him. I found his boat drifting off Beluga reef."

"He said it sank," Ascott said.

"It must have got better then."

"I guess."

"He's a bit weird, eh?" Shoal said, scowling at the oarlock on the side of her boat.

"Why? What did he say to you?"

"He turned up on the weekly flight from the city and said he was looking for Ascott Pudding."

"He found me," Ascott said again, and stowed the box at the pointy end of the canoe.

"You don't look like someone who's been publicly flogged and had their ears chewed off by rabid leeches."

Ascott straightened up. "He said that?"

"Yeah. I tried to start a betting pool on how disfigured you'd end up if he found you."

"He punched me in the nose," Ascott said.

"That's it?"

"It was enough to get his point across."

"Shipspit. That means I owe Curby two yellow pearls."

"So how much did you end up making from the betting pool?"

"Nothing, Curby was the only one willing to place a bet. Everyone else is too busy preparing for the whale race."

The whale race. Every year, vast pods of whales passed through the archipelago, their numbers so great that the Montabanians held an annual race where competitors would travel across tracts of ocean by running along the behemoths' backs.

"Entries still open?" Ascott asked.

"Yeah, till the end of the week, or until the first sighting. You gonna enter?" Shoal regarded him with an appraising eye.

"Hah, no."

"I'm entering this year." Shoal gave a slight tilt of her chin.

"It seems dangerous to the point of being suicidal," Ascott said.

"Only if you don't win."

"Well, thanks for the pizzas," Ascott said.

The pause that followed went so far beyond pregnant it saw its offspring graduate high school.

Finally Shoal regarded Ascott with amused eyes that matched the impossible blue of the sea. "Did you find anything new?"

"Zyngus eating aphish."

Shoal gave a snort. "Why is it that just because you haven't seen something before, you assume that no one else has ever seen it either?"

"It's science. I'm writing—"

"A book, yes, I know." Shoal rolled her eyes. "Take the day off and come fishing with me." She managed to make the invitation sound like an order.

"Sure, I guess. I'll just drop the pizzas back."

Shoal secured a towline to the bow of Ascott's canoe. The outboard motor on her skiff hummed and they jetted across the azure water and into the lagoon, bringing both boats to rest on the white sand of the beach.

Tacus hopped from foot to foot, crumbs of chewed crayon spraying across the table. He flapped his wings, his brightly coloured feathers spreading. "Thoal! Thoal!" he squawked.

"Hey Tacus, how's my favourite little fella?" Shoal scratched under the parrot's chin with one finger, making him purr deep in his throat.

Ascott put the pizzas in the empathically powered freezer. He had switched the voice reminder function off. The idea of his fridge talking to him did not appeal.

"Bithcuith!" Tacus demanded. Ascott handed Shoal a box of crackers. She took one and broke it into pieces, letting Tacus take them from her fingertips with dainty bites.

They left Ascott's canoe on the beach and took Shoal's boat on the fishing trip. Two spear guns lay along the bottom of the craft, four-foot-long poles with thick rubber bands that stretched back along their length. When released, the thin harpoon that lay along the pole shot forward and into the target. Shoal could kill anything with her practiced arm. She caught more fish with a spear than with a net or line.

Ascott left the snorkel in his canoe because Shoal always rolled her eyes if anyone suggested using SCRAM gear or even a snorkel. Watching her steer the boat as they zoomed across the lagoon, he wondered if she had gill slits hidden behind her ears.

Urged on with a few kind words to the empathically powered outboard motor, the boat zipped through the gap in the reef and out into open water. Ascott turned so he faced forward, his back to the girl steering the boat. Watching the vast plain of the warm ocean allowed him time to think about Charlotte and what he could do.

The boat purred to a halt on the vast, flat plain of gently rolling water. Peering over the side, Ascott saw fish going about their business. He wondered if they pondered the alien world above the way humans peered up at the unreachable stars.

"Have you ever thought we should be trying to communicate with them?" he said.

"With who?" Shoal lifted one of the spear guns off the bottom of the boat and sighted along the shaft of the harpoon.

"The fish. We could teach them so much about the world above."

"You're weird," Shoal announced and slipped into the water, spear in one hand and a catch bag in the other. With a single flick of her legs she sped downwards, a thin line of bubbles trailing behind her. Ascott took a deep breath, and then remembered that he would be expected to bring the second spear gun. He exhaled and picked it up. The head on the harpoon was razor sharp, with barbs like dagger points. Holding it carefully he dropped over the side. Shoal already had two fish; as he swam downwards she slid the corpses off the back of her harpoon and into the catch bag.

Feeling queasy, Ascott gave her the thumbs up. She shook her head and nodded a fist at him. Ascott waved his fist back at her, remembering that a thumbs-up meant *I need to surface,* not *Okay.*

Shoal darted off, her legs together and flexing like one long fin. Feeling guilty, Ascott swam after her. Shoal speared another fish, a large *gope,* which Ascott knew had a stable relationship with the mouth crab, a shell-less crustacean that lived in the fish's mouth and snacked on scraps of food passing through to the gullet. There was no evidence that it was a symbiotic pairing. Ascott's current theory was that the crabs were parasites and only remained in the gope's mouths because of a lack of fish dentists.

Shoal swam out into deeper water; Ascott trailed her for a while longer and then pushed up for the surface. Taking a breath, he trod water and waited for her to pop up.

When you are treading water in the middle of the ocean, a minute can seem like a long time. Two minutes feels like an eternity. After a minute and a half Ascott took a deep breath and dived down to see where Shoal had gone, the spear gun in his hand as superfluous as a centipede's walking stick.

With long strokes of his arms and legs, he cut through the water, reaching the bottom and then pulling himself along over rocks and bulbous corals, looking for the familiar mop of blonde hair as he went.

He saw it then, mostly buried in the sand and encrusted with coral—the kind of regular shape that nature doesn't bother with. The momentary distraction passed and he swam on; even a strong swimmer like Shoal could get in trouble. After swimming in a wide circle Ascott surfaced, took a deep breath and went down again. The cross shape, sticking out of the sand at an odd angle and covered in coral growth, was his starting point. Beyond it, he saw the dark outline of an old wooden ship, heavy with coral and seaweed that waved in the currents like green hair.

With the warning fire in his lungs beginning to rise, he swam deeper, pulling himself to the edge of the wreck and peering inside.

Chunks of the hull had rotted away, and the coral's steady advance over anything that wasn't fast enough to swim away had already engulfed most of the old timbers. It was dark in there and Ascott's lungs were insisting he take them somewhere nice, a place where fruit cocktails come with umbrellas and the air is free.

Letting go of the mouldering edge of the wreck, Ascott prepared to swim upwards. A surge of pale *something* burst out of the wreck and shot skyward. Ascott screamed. The last of his air gushing out of his mouth, Ascott scrambled for the surface, inhaling salt water that burned like fire.

Stars exploded, and the steel band around his chest cinched tighter. Ascott flailed, his arms and legs losing strength and coordination. As he rose towards the light, everything around him grew steadily darker.

CHAPTER 3

The aphish crawled along the wide expanse of the seaweed, its tiny circular mouth scraping a groove in the marinated surface of the flesh-like frond. A swirl of current washed over the tiny shell and it gripped tighter with its mouth parts, clinging to the only home it had ever known, to no avail.

Torn from the salty flesh, the aphish felt itself rolling over, larger mouthparts pressed against its coiled shell as something tried to slither in and suck the life right out of its calcified exoskeleton. The aphish struggled against the probing, and then life flowed in instead of out. Ascott broke the surface of consciousness and coughed hard, the splash of salt water heaving out of his lungs burning his throat again.

He floated on his back, Shoal tangled around his head and shoulders, her upside-down face regarding him with concern.

"Thought you might've checked out," she said. Ascott closed his eyes against the bright sunshine and felt the warm water carrying him.

"I lost you," he croaked.

"No, you nearly drowned yourself. I knew exactly where I was."

Ascott didn't argue. Every muscle ached and his throat felt like a sword-swallower's who had sneezed at the wrong moment.

"So, are we going to float here all day?" Ascott opened his eyes again at Shoal's voice. He became aware that she was holding him, keeping him afloat, and had breathed life into his drowned lungs.

"It's nice," he offered. "We should go drowning more often."

Shoal gave a snort. "You're useless at it. All that flailing and panicking."

"I just need more practice." Ascott lifted his head away from Shoal and got himself floating upright. Treading water, he turned to face her. "Got enough fish?"

"Sure. Did you see that wreck?"

Ascott nodded. "You went inside?"

"Yeah, it's the fruit."

"The fruit?"

"Yeah, it's fruity, you know, the best."

Ascott nodded again. "The fruitiest fruit."

Shoal pulled down the edge of the boat that floated behind her. Reaching in she retrieved a milknut with a stick jammed in the shell hole. Pulling the twig out with her teeth, she spat it away and handed the nut to Ascott. "Drink," she said.

He did. The sweet watery milk inside the hairy brown shell soothed his throat and when it was empty, he gasped for air.

"Better?" Shoal asked with a wry smile.

Ascott nodded and dropped the empty shell back in the boat.

"We should head back," Shoal said. With an easy grace she gripped the side of the skiff and launched herself out of the water and onto the flat deck. Ascott followed suit, the long drink of milknut juice rolling in his stomach as the boat nearly swamped.

Shoal started the motor and Ascott focused on not throwing up as they zipped across the waves back to his island and the three-room, bamboo-construction, solar-powered, minimal-plumbing, palm-leaf-roofed house of Pudding.

"You gonna be okay?" Shoal asked after the boat beached itself on the white sand. Ascott nodded and waved away the offered fish.

"Pizza's fine," he mumbled.

"Take a nap," Shoal suggested. Ascott nodded again, pushing the boat out and returning Shoal's farewell wave as she gunned the motor and headed out across the lagoon.

"Bithcuith!" Tacus demanded from his position on the veranda table.

Ascott sighed. *Actually* drowning in Shoal's company would have been preferable to nearly drowning. At least then he wouldn't have to live with the embarrassment of it.

"Thoal!" Tacus demanded.

"You and me both, buddy," Ascott replied. He put three crackers on the table and heated a pizza while the parrot dissected each biscuit in turn with his beak.

He ate pizza and stared with self-critical frustration at the few clothes tossed into the open suitcase, still lying where he had left it hours before. *Charlotte,* Ascott reminded himself. *I have to do something.*

What to do was the question. In the eighteen months since he left his parents' house for the last time, Ascott had only sent one postcard. He couldn't keep in touch with his only surviving family member even before he knew she was dying. Guilt gnawed at him the pointless way Kibblefish nibbled on small rocks.

Sleep came uneasily to him that night and Ascott dreamed of being underwater. Rainbows of fish spiralled around him, all of them whispering in tones too low to be understood. From the grey-green-skinned *flamets* to the iridescent flash of the *kabris*, the denizens of the sea came in the full range of colours. The shapes were as varied as the hues, from arrow thin *sprax* to the wide sail bodied *veskas*. Ascott swam with the fish and yearned to communicate with them.

On cue, Shoal appeared in his dream, her long tanned legs effortlessly sweeping through the water, driving her towards him. Ascott watched as Shoal metamorphosed into an unknown fish.

What separated this recurring dream from a nightmare was that Ascott found the half-girl, half-fish Shoal fascinating. He longed to study her habits and swim as freely as she did in the warm waters of the blue-green sea. The fantasy was a familiar one and Ascott floated, smiling and at peace. Then, from the corner of his eye, he saw a figure in white trousers and shirt striding along the coral outcrop of a nearby reef, the currents tugging and lifting the hems of his shirt and trouser cuffs. Ascott turned his dreaming eyes and stared at the intruder.

Drakeforth held up a white memo board, on which he had written: *May I have a word?*

Ascott found himself nodding in his dream, the water swirling around him, the fish dancing their intricate ballet, so far beyond his understanding.

Drakeforth waved the fish away as if they were buzzing flies. With a marker pen, he wrote something else on his board and turned it back to show Ascott.

This is bigger than fish. This is everything.

Ascott waved his hands; the fish were everything. Charlotte was everything. Drakeforth scrubbed the board clean and wrote again.

Where do we come from? What are we really?

Ascott shook his head. The questions were interrupting his time with Shoal and the other fish.

A sharp pain shot through Ascott's earlobe. He flailed and sat up with a yell: *"Tacus!"* The parrot hopped from foot to foot on the bed cover, eyeing Ascott sideways with his usual air of innocence.

"Athleep on watch! Flog him!" Tacus declared. Ascott groaned and fell back. The sunlight now streaming in through the windows said morning had come around again. He didn't feel rested. His hair follicles ached. A cup of tea on the veranda would be the cure for that.

Tacus met him at the table, the parrot deftly opening the box of crayons and selecting a worn green stick. The sheets of paper he drew on were weighed down with beach stones. Ascott put some crackers on a plate and sipped his tea while Tacus tried to decide whether to draw or eat breakfast. Drawing won out for now. The bird positioned the crayon in his beak and, with one eye cocked to stare at the paper, he began to draw.

Ascott munched on cold pizza. It had vegetables on it, so he guessed he was getting a balanced diet. The tea supposedly contained enough nutritional vitamins and minerals to bring the dead back to life.

"Pitheth of fate!" Tacus declared, and dropped the blue crayon in favour of a red.

Ascott took a fatherly interest in the parrot's artwork. Tacus sometimes laboured over a masterpiece for several days, always drawing in crayon and only drawing in lines, lacking, Ascott thought, the dexterity to fill in the shapes he drew.

"Bithcuith," Tacus announced, pushing the completed picture aside with his four-toed foot. Ascott fed him a broken cracker while reviewing the latest drawing. Like most of the parrot's artworks it was a green blob, with odd marks and random notations floating around inside it.

"That's a very nice amoeba, Tacus."

"Everyone'th a critic," Tacus squawked. Once an artwork was complete to his satisfaction, the parrot lost all interest in it and went on to the next one. Sometimes he drew triangular shapes, like mountains. Other times he drew stick figures of trees and animals. Mostly he drew amoeba-like blobs with different-coloured organelles adrift within the green, yellow or red membrane.

"Do you want me to put it on the fridge?" Ascott asked.

"Bithcuith!"

Ascott finished his tea and pizza. He had no idea when the next flight would leave Montaban's tiny airport—which was really more of a seaport, with a single zipillin tower for the airships to tether to. Ascott thought they might fly out once a week, but island time was relative, like a third cousin twice removed. He finished packing, the suitcase lighter than he remembered and the guilt heavier.

Ascott collected the SCRAM gear from the closet. He didn't need much. An inflatable harness, air-tanks, regulator, weight belt and a second belt from which to hang useful things like a knife, torch and catch bags. He might have a chance for one last dive before he left the islands forever. Either way, Shoal could keep it for him until he came back, one day.

Ascott carried the dive gear down to the dugout. Above sea level the weight of the gear was staggering; only when you were in the water, and the change in density supported all the extra baggage, did it feel like flying. The diving equipment gave him an almost endless range to swim, observe, and explore. Ascott didn't care what Shoal said—every time he went under water and saw some new rock, or coral or fish, it gave him a complete sense of discovery. The ocean life might not be new to her, but when he saw something for the first time, there was always the chance he might be the first person to see it. That sense of achievement balanced against everything else in his life that felt like failure.

Montaban was too far away to paddle, so he retrieved the outboard motor from the closet, too. After bolting it in place and waking it up gently with a round of positive affirmations, he got the motor going. Tacus tipped a rock onto his current art project and flapped down to land in the bow of the canoe.

"Montaban or butht!" the parrot declared, spreading his wings to catch the morning sun.

The canoe cut through the water like an arrow shot from a bow specifically modified to send small boats skimming across the ocean for great distances. The hum of the engine and the occasional indignant squawk from Tacus as a wave splashed his feathers were the only sounds as they zipped over the blue surface. Ascott thought about how similar to a desert the sea appeared. Both seemed featureless, shaped by wind and the movement of the particles. But the ocean, Ascott mused, is not a desert. It's more like a border; a line between two worlds, each as vast, complex and self-sustaining as the other. Only a very few specialised creatures could live in both worlds. If given the choice, Ascott would be hard pressed to decide which one he would prefer to live in permanently. He knew he would follow the fish to the ends of the earth—or the bottom of the ocean if necessary. The thought that gnawed at him like an aphish on seaweed was: did it matter that the fish didn't care?

This brought him back to Earth with a thud that matched the pounding of the canoe as it crested a swell and dropped into the following trough.

Montaban clung to the limestone and ancient coral sands of an island in the western end of the Aardvark Archipelago. A modern settlement had been here for two hundred years, started by sailors deciding that life on a well-resourced island in the middle of a tropical ocean was better than crewing trade ships for a pittance wage and a diet of worm-infested scones.

The native people had been here, in their language, forever. The locals had watched with baffled amusement as the men who abandoned their ships (in some instances sinking them first) struggled to survive on one of the more barren of the archipelago's islands. After a few months, it was decided that they go and check on the new neighbours. The welcoming committee reported back that some of the men had died from eating things a child would know to avoid, while others had taken to wearing palm-fronds and milknut half-shells and insisting they be called *Shelley*. A vote was taken and the survivors were rescued. After a few good meals and sleep in a proper hammock, the ex-sailors admitted they had no idea a thriving civilisation was going about its business only a couple of islands away.

From then on, the thousand islands of the Aardvark Archipelago had been mostly ignored, except by those who lived on them. In due course the militant missionary expeditions of Arthurians like Saint Amoeba and Saint Kebab gave the woefully stagnant gene pool the equivalent of a good dose of chlorine, a thorough vacuum, and a skim with a leaf scoop in the form of new settlers. The Arthurians took their missionary positions seriously and set about populating Montaban with the children of good, Arthur-worshipping people. The Montabanians didn't suffer any of the tragic cultural misunderstandings of some other indigenous tribes when faced with the infamous choice of Saint Kebab.* They readily abandoned their casual pantheon of gods based on natural phenomena and fish-spirit worship in return

---

* Kebab's Choice: when a blood-stained lunatic holds a sword to your throat and asks if you have thought about abandoning your current false dogma for the up-and-coming, one true religion of Arthurianism. It proved to be a remarkably successful crusade and Saint Kebab's campaign ran at a conversion rate of nearly a hundred per cent. It would have been a perfect score, except due to an unfortunate cultural misunderstanding with the Took people, who lived on the wild and windswept tundra plateau of Upper Besex. The Took shook their heads when they wanted to indicate yes.

for the promise of one-ness with the Universal Perception that, if Drakeforth was not completely deluded, had since retired in a petulant sulk.

Montaban today counted several thousand people living in houses made of carved limestone blocks. These were made, in most cases, by cutting the blocks out of the ancient sea cliffs and then calling the resulting cave a three-bedroom bungalow with indoor—outdoor flow and unobstructed sea-views. The stone blocks went into patio construction and walls to keep out the worst of the neighbours' cooking smells. Narrow streets wound around the rocky island the way sheep paths form contour-lines on hill pasture.

The Montabanians shared their town with the cats. No one had ever counted the number of cats living in Montaban, except to note that they were abundant. In the way of cats, they kept to themselves and barely acknowledged the people as they accepted tribute in the form of fish-scraps.

Ascott slowed the boat as they passed through the outer limits of the moored fishing fleet. Boats of all shapes and sizes bobbed in the wake of the canoe's passing. Line trawlers, net draggers, wooden skiffs like Shoal's, and the controversial bang boats that discharged static electricity into the water before scooping up the stunned fish, blanketed the surface leading up to the docks and beach.

"Varletth! Thcow-baggerth! Muck muncherth!" Tacus squawked at each boat that zoomed and zipped through the fray, sending water splashing over the spluttering parrot.

Ascott shushed the bird and flicked the outboard engine off as they drifted towards the public dock. Tying the canoe up, he offered a hand for Tacus to step on to. From there the parrot walked sideways up his arm and took position on his shoulder.

"Don't trutht the catth," Tacus muttered.

"Okay," Ascott said and Tacus settled like a broody hen, apparently content that his warning had been heeded.

The docks of Montaban seethed with fishermen, fishmongers, fishwives, fish-scavenging birds and the occasional octopus that had picked the lock on its aquarium cage and was making a break for the freedom of open water.

After months of solitude on his unnamed island, the crowds were as deafening to Ascott as the fish-stink was cloying. He lifted the two air tanks on to the dock and climbed up. The fugitive octopus slipped past, warning Ascott away with a knife fashioned from a sharpened piece of coral clutched in one desperate tentacle.

Tacus threw himself into the air, landing heavily on his shoulder.

"You can fly, you know," Ascott said, gritting his teeth against the stabbing pain above his collarbone.

Tucking one air tank under each arm, Ascott walked past baskets of fresh fish, milknuts, dried fruit, shellfish, and a chap selling driftwood that looked like it had wizened faces in the grain. In Montaban if you weren't selling something, you were a customer, and everyone offered Ascott their wares. Pearls were the official currency, with different colours denoting different values. They ranged from the common black pearls through to the highly valued reds that glowed like the sunset over an approaching hurricane.

Ascott plunged through the crowd, holding his breath when the smell became too much and ignoring the constant cries of "Very best deal on queen shrimp! Fresh caught today!".

The office of the Montaban Export Company acted as the seat of power in the port town. It was also the town hall, bank, Arthurian church, safe-deposit, legal records office, and guardian of Montaban's only working telephone. Ascott wondered if it ever rang, seeing as no one else in this part of the ocean had a phone. The Exco was the largest building at dock level and had been built from a mixture of local limestone block and imported sheet-metal roofing, some of which was even on the roof.

Ascott left the two air tanks outside and ventured into the cool gloom where he joined a queue of locals in front of a barred teller's window. The lobby had the same cave-like interior as other buildings in Montaban. It vibrated with the chatter of people, and the noises of their livestock, except for the fish, who were either hanging from lines threaded through their gills, or swimming around in large glass jars and not talking to anyone.

There were no signs to suggest he was in the right place to buy a ticket home, but the line of people ahead of him, and quickly growing behind him, gave the impression of important business.

In time Ascott reached the window. On the other side of the counter, a wizened and grey-haired gent with skin as tanned as a milknut, wearing a starched collar and bowtie (but no shirt), enquired as to the nature of his business.

"I'd like to buy a ticket, to Kulo—I mean, The City," Ascott said.

"Pitheth o' fate!" Tacus squawked. "Give uth your money!"

"A ticket?" The grey-haired teller leaned closer, tilting his head and giving Ascott the same one-eyed, disbelieving expression Tacus often did.

"Yes, I need to go home. My sister is in trouble," Ascott tried again.

"Next flight, is in a few days," the teller said. "Ticket costs…" He examined a stained page, brittle with age. "Two greens and five blues."

Ascott floundered. "Pearls? Uh, what's the exchange rate?"

"The what?"

"Bithcuith! Bury 'em deep!" Tacus called.

Ascott felt the colour rising in his face. The people in the line behind him were watching with good-natured amusement, but that couldn't last. He risked a look back; his fellow queue-ees held braces of fish, cages of live chickens, island pigs on string leashes and baskets of ripe fruit. Two cats were sitting in a stream of sunshine, and he was sure they were laughing at him too.

"Do you accept credit stick transfers in exchange for pearls?" Ascott said, his voice hoarse with anxiety.

"Well now…that's a good question…" The teller turned left and then right in his seat. Finally seeing what he sought, he slid carefully off his chair and walked with slow determination over to an ancient filing cabinet. "Open up now," he said, and patted the wood affectionately.

The filing cabinet shivered and gave a snort. Ascott felt a pang of remembrance. Charlotte loved living oak furniture.

Sliding open the top cabinet, the teller retrieved a heavy, leather-bound tome. Pushing the drawer shut, he blew a thick layer of dust off the book. Tottering under the weight he returned and set it down on the counter. The ancient pages creaked as they were turned.

"Ah, here we are," he said eventually. Ascott craned his neck and could make out the faded lettering of the archaic script: *Raytes o' Xchaynge Fo' Foryne Coyne.*

The teller regarded the tiny lettering for a moment and then paused to retrieve a pair of reading spectacles. In the growing queue behind him, Ascott heard one of the pigs sigh.

"A yellow pearl shall be exchanged for a sum of...No, I can't quite make that out. Let's see...Two black pearls shall be exchanged for a quark. How many quarks do you have?" The teller looked at Ascott over his glasses.

"Quarkth! Quarkth!" Tacus squawked, sounding like an asthmatic duck.

"I don't have any quarks." Ascott wished a freak wave would immediately crash into the building, at best destroying all trace of his ever being here, and at worst giving the spectators something other than the back of his head to stare at.

The teller gave a nasal *Hmm* and went back to perusing the fine print.

"Never mind, I'll come back later. With a pig or some chickens or—something." Ascott stared down the narrow tunnel of light that his vision had reduced to and put the doorway in the centre of it. Marching forward he tripped over a dozing pig, which squealed and sent him stumbling into a woman with a brown hen in a cage, one of which promptly laid an egg on the floor.

The pandemonium of the dockside was a relief after escaping the chaos of the Exco. Tacus sat hunched and silent on Ascott's shoulder as he gathered up the two dive tanks and wondered if Vole Drakeforth could help him.

A man in black jeans, black sunglasses and a white t-shirt interrupted Ascott's reverie. "I couldn't help but notice the trouble you had at the Exco and I wanted to say, that's quite the bird you have there, my friend."

"Tell me about it," Ascott said, trying to breathe his anxious pulse back to a normal rate after the fiasco in the Exco

"What's your name, bird?" The man asking had a casual air of coolness about him. He wasn't local; his clothes, haircut and demeanour suggested that he viewed Montaban as an exotic stop-over, a mere point of interest in his otherwise busy and cool life. His arms were a rainbow of tattoos, mostly showing sailing ships being hugged by humungous squid with the same single-minded focus of a drunk seducing girls on the dance floor of a nightclub.

"Tacuth," Tacus squawked, and then shied away as the man reached out to stroke his feathers with one ring-strewn hand.

"Tacuth?" the man said.

"Tacus. I didn't name him. He has trouble with his esses. But he is a very intelligent bird." Ascott wished the stranger would move on; the attention was making him uncomfortable.

"That is so true, my friend. People underestimate the intelligence of birds. Parrots live for a long time, too. They see a lot and they remember everything."

"Bilge puppy," Tacus said.

"He talks a lot of nonsense," Ascott explained.

"He could live to be over one hundred years old," the stranger said, his voice as smooth and coiling as a sea snake. "Barring accidents," he added.

"I think he used to be a ship's parrot. He often uses nautical terms," Ascott said.

"Very likely. You know there have been pirates, privateers and smugglers in these waters for generations?"

Ascott nodded. He had heard the stories of legends like Noodle Basket Nung, Three-Eyed Petunia and The Bosun of Backwash, all said to be ruthless pirates who died with secret treasure buried on hidden islands somewhere in the archipelago.

"Not these days, though," Ascott said. The revolution of empathic technology over a century ago had changed the world in many ways. Reducing the need for people to transport their valuables by woefully under-insured sailing ships was just one of the benefits of Godden's discovery.

"Ascott Pudding," Ascott said and set the air-tanks down before extending a hand.

"Kalim Aari." They shook hands and smiled in that polite way strangers do for form's sake. "My friends call me Kal."

"Did you come on a tourist ship, Kal?" Ascott racked his mind for suitable small talk. There was no weather to speak of in the islands. Either it was warm and dry with clear skies, or it was hurricane season. Commenting on the weather was generally considered in poor taste, as it was blindingly obvious that either it was a nice day, or your house had just exploded under the onslaught of 200-mile-an-hour winds.

"Kalim," Kalim replied.

"Sorry?" Ascott backtracked on his mental diversion to see what he had missed.

"My friends call me Kal," the stranger repeated and smiled in an, *I wish there was something I could do, but that's how it is*, kind of way.

"Did you come in on a cruise ship...? Kalim?" Ascott tried again.

"No. I'd like to buy your parrot. How much do you want for him?" Kalim reached into his shirtfront and extracted a leather pouch of soft fish-skin that bulged like the cheeks of a bulimic squirrel. He hefted it in his palm, setting the pearls inside clinking against each other.

"He's not for sale," Ascott said while his brain gaped at his stupidity.

"Name your price." The bag of pearls chattered in Kalim's hand.

"I can't. There isn't one." Ascott picked up the air tanks, stepped around Kalim and started to walk away. The stranger's hand clamped around his arm.

"Think of one. I want the bird," Kalim said in a voice with fangs and full-moon nights spent chained up in windowless cellar rooms in its tone. Tacus made a disapproving growl deep in his throat and fluffed his plumage.

Ascott jerked his arm free. "I can't help you. Technically, Tacus isn't even my bird. He just lives in my house, eats my food and draws pictures on my spare note-paper."

"What kind of pictures?" Kalim stepped closer, as if wary of being overheard.

"Amoeba, mostly." Ascott felt relief at the flash of confusion in Kalim's eyes. He took the opportunity to turn on his heel and push through the market crowd.

CHAPTER 4

Ascott scuttled along the narrow streets, paved in limestone gravel pounded flat by centuries of passing feet, and climbed towards the cliffs.

Supporting industries thrived up here in the limestone. The net weavers, the boat builders, and the seafood restaurants. Ascott followed a winding trail between the second and third tier of shops on the cliff until he came to a driftwood sign with the words *Smith Dive Emprm.* burned into it with a hot poker. There was no door, of course. There were very few doors in Montaban; they blocked the flow of cool air and customers.

"Hello?" Ascott said, stepping into the dark interior.

The walls of the shop cave were hung with the mummified and snarling carcasses of various monsters from the deep. Some were so cleverly done that you could barely see the stitching where mundane animals had suffered the final indignity of having their tanned hides reshaped into chimerical creations of fins and fangs. The rattle of a bead curtain announced the arrival of Palm Smith, entering the shop from the rear. She had the dark wavy hair of an Archipelago native and the blue eyes of a fertile Arthurian monk with recessive genes. Her whipcord body was wrapped in the lightweight, brightly coloured fabrics common to the islands. Over all it formed a loose skirt around the hips and a cross-over bandeau-style top half that left plenty of unobstructed access for the skin to breathe.

"Can I help you?" she asked.

"I wanted to talk to Shoal, please." Ascott set the tanks on the stone floor with a clunk.

"You're that crazy kid that Shoal is always talking about, eh?" Palm's eyes glowed in the dim light.

"I'm Ascott. I'm studying the fish of the islands."

"Yup, crazy as a purple pearl." Palm bustled forward, the bright colours of her skirt amplifying the rustle of the flapping fabric. She seized Ascott in her wiry tanned arms and hugged him to her chest. "You getting enough to eat? You look too thin. You should stay for lunch and dinner too, eh?"

"I really just wanted to talk to Shoal. I have, uhh, some diving to do." The unaccustomed hugging made Ascott glow with embarrassment.

"Sandy! Get out here and do some work, you useless fella!" Palm barked at the room beyond the bead curtain and then beamed beatifically at Ascott again. "Hubby'll take care of that for you right quick."

"Uhh, okay?" Ascott took a step back as Sandy Smith slipped into the shop from somewhere out back. He wore a frayed pair of cut-off shorts, a faded t-shirt, and bare feet. His long hair, the same shade of blonde as Shoal's, was tied back in thick, dreadlocked stalks like drying seaweed. His eyes were dark and warm.

"What's happenin' darlin'?" He patted Palm's behind and then noticed Ascott for the first time.

"Hey, man. Welcome to Smith's Dive Emporium. What can we interest you in?"

"He wants his tanks filled, and then he is staying for lunch," Palm said in a tone that would brook no disagreement.

"Most excellent. Most outstandin'…We runnin' a restaurant now?" Sandy looked around, a puzzled expression on his face. He looked as if he had been asleep for the winter and his wife's shouting had woken him from hibernation.

"This is Ascott, Shoal's friend from The City." Palm said 'friend' in a way that might be mistaken for 'future husband' in some dialects. Anyone not born in Montaban was considered to be from The City. A mythical place with cars, television and telephones, plural. The City was said to be so far from the ocean that some people went their whole lives without ever seeing it.

"Excellent, outstandin'. I'm Sandy, this is my wife Palm. Shoal's not here right now, man. She's, uhh…not here. Right now."

"That's okay. I just came to see Shoal. I'm leaving Montaban."

"Leaving? You just got here, man." Sandy threw his hands up and sprang forward. Seizing the tanks, he twisted them and peered at the regulator fittings at the top. "We can fill these tanks with sweet, sweet, air." Sandy inhaled a long shoulder wrenching breath through his nose and then exhaled slowly. "So sweet…we should bottle it and sell it to people. Which…" he added, realisation rising on his face like a spring tide, "…is just what we are doin'. Man, I love this job!" Sandy lifted the tanks easily and jogged out through the bead curtain. The steel tanks clanged on the stone floor and the thudding hiss of high-pressure air compressors started a few moments later.

"Shoal says you are writing a big book. You a University fella, eh?" Palm regarded Ascott with a mother's shrewd gaze.

"Well yes, it's an encyclopaedia. A reference guide to all the fish in the Aardvark Archipelago."

Palm grinned. "Why?" she asked.

"Because…because no one knows about the fish. The only fish most people see are the ones they eat. There are thousands of species of life out there in the reefs and lagoons and they are all waiting to be discovered."

"How do you know them fish are waiting to be discovered? Maybe they're living out there in the coral and the lagoons because they don't want to be discovered? You ever think of that, University fella?"

Ascott shook his head and took another step back towards the glaring white of the sun-struck limestone outside. He stumbled and lost his balance, almost falling into a brace of waveboards stacked against one wall. They slid aside, revealing a painted mural of a fat and happy-looking giant, brown-skinned man sitting cross-legged surrounded by milknut trees and laughing heartily.

Tacus screamed and leaped from Ascott's shoulder.

"He'th found uth! Bithcuith!" the parrot squawked.

"Tacus, come back here." Ascott hurried over and tried to encourage the bird back on to his hand. The bird landed on a high shelf, atop a sea urchin the size of a basketball that had shed its spines.

"Bothun! Boil my bilgeth!" Tacus scolded, hopping daintily sideways to avoid Ascott's grasp.

"Some things, they just want to be left alone. They nobody's business," Palm watched Ascott's desperate attempts to secure Tacus with apparent amusement.

"Thtow that fith!" Tacus spluttered. "Thplithe the mainthail! Turn uth about! Bumth to the hurricane boyth!"

"I'm very sorry," Ascott said, seizing Tacus around the body and wincing as the parrot's flapping wings knocked the balding seashell down.

"Maybe he wants to be outside, in the fresh air?" Palm suggested. Ascott hurried to the door and let Tacus take flight. The parrot beat his wings gamely and then perched on a nearby wall, exhausted from the struggle.

"Bad fith," he scolded.

"Bad parrot," Ascott warned. Tacus gave an indignant croak and ducked his head under a wing.

Ascott stepped back inside. Palm was gathering up the broken sea-urchin shell. "I'm really sorry. I can pay for any damage," he said.

"It's a blessing to see this thing get knocked down. I don't know why Sandy insists on keeping it." Palm regarded the thin ball of shell. "You know why the interior of these things is considered a delicacy in these parts?"

Ascott shook his head.

"It's because even if you are starving, something that tastes like ground-up fish guts mixed with sand needs a certain mystique to make people want to eat it."

Sandy emerged from the back room carrying the two considerably heavier air tanks.

"Here you go man, that'll be three blues a piece."

"Do you accept credit?" Ascott took the credit stick from his pocket. He had access to his parents' estate, at least his half of it, in an account. Shoal was the only person to have used it in the last eighteen months, for Ascott's living expenses like pizzas, clothes and SCRAM gear.

"Man, it's like invisible money. You don't see it, you don't touch it, it doesn't exist. Me, I like the click of pearls in my pocket, especially when they've got a nice glow on."

"There's only one place in Montaban that has a less than narrow-eyed, spit-on-your-shoe kind of suspicion about credit sticks," Palm said. "The Exco."

"I'm really sorry," Ascott said, his cheeks glowing in the ebony-hued gloom. "There's a problem at the Export Company, they don't seem to be able to help."

"No problem, you stay for lunch. Pay for the tank fill later." Palm waved his apology away.

"That's very kind of you," Ascott said, his voice cracking.

"You haven't tasted her cooking," Sandy muttered and then gave a yelp as Palm cuffed him upside the back of his head.

"Nothing wrong with my cooking," Palm declared.

Ascott found himself escorted through the back of the shop, past the air-tank compressor and dive gear repair workroom, up a set of stairs cut into the stone, and into an open-plan apartment above. The sea breeze wafted in through the open windows and stirred hanging mobiles of driftwood and wave-polished shells, which tinkled and reflected sunlight.

They ate traditional island fare of fish three ways: fried, baked and boiled. Each delicate serving came wrapped in a fragrant leaf that was peeled and used as a plate. Fruit and mashed root vegetables were the side dishes, notable for their non-fish flavours more than any differences in texture.

They drank java, a mildly fermented fizzy yeast drink traditionally made from mixing milknut juice and the tears of women mourning their men lost at sea. Nowadays the lost men could usually be found in one of the dockside bars, and the tears had been replaced by water exhumed from the Montaban reservoir through the town's antique and utterly mysterious plumbing system. Ascott enjoyed java, or *Cuppa Joe* as the locals also called it. It made his lips numb and his brain fizz.

Conversation flowed around the table, the Smiths listening with the polite but reserved interest of people sharing a dining table with an escaped mental patient as Ascott explained his mission to catalogue the sea-life of the Aardvarks.

"Whatcha gonna do with this book. When you've finished it?" Sandy asked while peeling a red, the blood-coloured juice dripping down his hands.

"Write another one," Ascott said. Sandy nodded, splitting the red into segments and sucking the sweet nectar from his fingers.

"What's that one going to be about?" Palm asked, offering another leaf laden with a whole baked fish that Ascott declined with a shake of his head.

"I'm not sure. I might try writing fiction stories."

"What kind of animal is that?" Sandy asked.

"It's not an animal you old fool," Palm scolded. "It's made up stories with romance and action and adventure and villains."

"Oh...I'd stick with the ones about fish," Sandy said.

"What about pirates?" Ascott asked. Palm and Sandy exchanged a glance.

"No pirates around here," Palm said firmly.

"Not anymore. Not like when we was kids, eh Palm?" Sandy grinned.

"I remember when the Seaguard went out and hunted down Captain Aarrgh. He'd been attacking boats and raiding fishing villages around the islands. They reckon he was looking for pirate treasure and went crazy."

"He went crazy from searching for a lost treasure?" Ascott said and sipped his java.

Palm shook her head. "No, boy, he went crazy "cos he found it."

Ascott frowned. "The treasure drove him mad?"

"It could have been heatstroke and dehydration," Sandy said. "The stories vary."

"There used to be a lot of pirates in the Aardvarks, right?" Ascott asked.

"Yeah. This fella was a descendent of the original Captain

Aarrgh, famous pirate in these parts," Palm began to clear the table of the empty leaves.

"People say the first Captain Aarrgh found a fabulous treasure. But his boat sank with all hands lost before he could tell anyone what he did with it, or where it was buried. People still go off looking for it and everything else that's been buried out there. If all the stories were true, you couldn't dig for chums on any beach without unearthing a treasure chest bursting with stolen loot." Sandy held the small white shell of a cooked chum up between two fingers to illustrate his point.

Ascott sat back with a satisfied sigh and a contended belch. ""Scuse me," he mumbled. "I should get going," he added, quickly standing up and trying not to stretch too much.

"Catht off!" Tacus announced from where he had been sulking on the window sill. He bobbed up and down until Ascott lifted him up to his shoulder perch.

"I'll give you a hand with the tanks." Sandy climbed out from the table and led Ascott down the stairs.

Ascott trailed behind him as Sandy lifted the two tanks and walked to the door, only to stop as a shadow filled the doorway.

"Hey man," Sandy said. "How can I help?"

"I need some tanks filled and I need some information."

Ascott froze as he recognised Kalim Aarl's voice.

"Here." Sandy handed a tank back to Ascott, who nearly buckled under the weight.

"Tank fills is three blues a piece. Information, well, that's a different scale."

"The tanks are on my boat. I'll have them brought up. I'm told there's a local historian that lives here."

"Is that right?" Sandy frowned.

Ascott stepped out of the shadows. "Hello again, Kalim."

"Mr Pudding." Kalim still wore the large black sunglasses that hid his eyes. "I'm interested in facts—not stories, mind, but facts about historical shipwrecks in the islands."

Sandy lifted the other air tank and scratched his nose with one finger of the same hand. Ascott marvelled at the casual strength of the man.

"Plenty of shipwrecks out there. Hidden reefs, bad storms, giant octopuses, shrimp that'll eat the hull right out from under you. Lot of ways to wreck a boat." Sandy spoke with the authority of one who believes what he says to be undisputed fact. "Anyway, Palm knows more about this stuff than I do." Sandy went to the bead curtain and yelled up the stairs. Palm came down, drying her hands on a towel.

"Fella wants to ask you some stuff about shipwrecks," Sandy waved at Kalim. "I'll give the boy a hand with the tanks." He swung the air tank over his shoulder and marched out the door. Ascott quickly followed, feeling the stranger's dark glasses turning to stare at his back.

CHAPTER 5

"Don't go diving for at least another hour after eating," Sandy said as they laid the tanks down in the bottom of the canoe. Ascott agreed he would not and they climbed back up the ladder to the dock. Tacus hopped off Ascott's shoulder and settled at the front of the boat, ready to hurl abuse and navigational advice once they were under way.

"Have you ever seen that guy in the sunglasses before?" Ascott said.

"Nah, probably arrived on one of the seasonal fishing ships, or flew in. We call them *tourists*."

"I met him before. He wanted to buy Tacus."

"What, like some bird seed or something?"

"No, he wanted to buy the parrot. Take him off my hands. Said to name my price."

"People these days, always so ready to sell things. Trust me, if there weren't a good reason to be bottling air and selling it to people, I'd be just as happy to give it away. But that Palm, she has plans. Wants Shoal to go to college and see something other than ocean in her life."

"College isn't that great," Ascott said with feeling. "Mostly it's sitting in a big room full of people being told what to think and believe, but no one really explains why you should think that way or believe those things."

"They do a college course yet that teaches you how to be happy?" Sandy asked with a grin.

"Not that I've seen." Ascott looked grim.

"Not much point in signin' up then, eh? If you want to learn things, read a book like yours, or talk to people. Plenty of them around these parts. Some of them know more than they're letting on. Other ones are just passing through so fast that you're not sure you should be sayin' hi or bye. Let alone askin' their name."

"I'm not going to sell Tacus, not for anything. Especially to some stranger." Ascott felt as certain of that as he had of anything in a long time.

"Course you ain't. It'd be like me trying to sell the air. The air ain't for sale, neither's a bird, or a wave, or a tree. They're just doin' their own thing and we're there to appreciate it."

"You sell air for three blue pearls a tank," Ascott said.

"Not quite." Sandy tapped the side of his nose with one long leathery finger. "I sell the service of fillin' up the tanks. The air is free. The mechanical compression, that's what you're payin' for."

Sandy started laughing and Ascott found himself laughing with him. They laughed until tears ran down the furrows in Sandy's cheeks and he collapsed on the dock timber clutching his sides. Ascott slowly recovered his breath, though he couldn't explain what was funny. Maybe the humour was contagious. Something deep inside let go and he laughed till he gasped.

"Hey," he said nudging the wheezing Sandy, "Is that Shoal's boat?" He pointed at a flat-bottomed skiff, the prow pointing skyward at a 45 degree angle while a high white plume of wash shot out the back. The outboard motor hurtled the wooden torpedo into the tangle of the Montaban local fleet. It zipped past the other canoes, coracles, cruisers, crab-boats, catch-craft and the occasional wind-surfer. A flash of blonde hair came into view on some of the turns as Sandy squinted into the glare.

"What's got her so excited?" he muttered. Shoal was waving and the only thing stopping her from standing up was the angle of the deck and the need to keep one hand on the throttle. With a *whoosh* and a sudden coughing gurgle from the outboard, she arrived at the dock, cut the engine power and leapt for the ladder.

Sandy and Ascott crowded around as her head popped up. "Whales!" she gasped, her eyes glowing with excitement.

"What, already?" Sandy said.

"Oh yeah, a whole pod of them, maybe twelve veterans and a few first-timers."

Sandy slapped his thigh and did an impromptu jig. "Goosegonegoggles!" he exclaimed. "I'm gonna ring the bell!" He took off running up the dock, vanishing into the market crowd. Ascott extended a hand and helped Shoal up the last rungs of the ladder.

"The migration has started?" he asked.

"Migration started a month ago, maybe two." Shoal was breathless with excitement. "They swim a long way from down south to reach us. They come up to the islands to have babies and next year they'll all come back."

"So the race...?" Ascott wished he had been less focused on his own misery a year ago and had paid more attention to local news and traditions.

"Will be in a few days. These are just the first whales. Soon there'll be so many coming through the deep channel that they'll block the way for shipping and then the race will happen."

Ascott wanted to ask more questions, but at that moment a bell started ringing somewhere up by the Exco. An urgent, joyous pealing echoed out over the island. Silence fell over the market and then it was as if all Montaban took a deep breath and shouted at once: "WHALES!"

A spontaneous carnival atmosphere erupted across the dock and surrounding town. People cheered, screamed and shouted. Bands struck up a discordant song and it sounded like it could be a while before they all came round to playing the same tune with the same timing, in the same key.

"Shoal, I need to go home. Back to The City," Ascott said while Shoal jumped up and down and cheered along with the others.

"What?!" she shouted over the noise.

"I'm going to dive that wreck we found, with SCRAM gear. I need to find some pearls so I can pay for a ticket home. "

"Why?"

Ascott wanted to say that he felt that Drakeforth had given him a message that he couldn't ignore. But the prospect of explaining about Charlotte, and his own anxiety about everything, muted Ascottt for a moment. Instead he shouted, "Because it might be home to fish I haven't seen before. I'll need to catalogue them for the encyclopaedia!"

"Ever seen a whale?" Shoal shouted back.

"Well, no, but they'll be here for a while. I don't imagine that they are leaving again today!"

"This is important!" Shoal's face darkened.

"So is this diving trip. I want you to come with me!" he added.

"We can go out there any time! It's carnival! The whales are here!"

"Great! I'll go on my own, then!" Ascott threw his hands up in the air.

"Diving alone is dangerous!" Shoal snapped.

"And running along the backs of whales isn't?"

"Is that what this is about? You don't think I can do it?!"

"I think you are crazy! I think that anyone who tries it risks getting killed!"

A heaving mob of singing dancers twirled along the dock, sweeping up everyone in their path. Ascott stepped back to the edge to avoid being caught in the crowd. Shoal followed him, her face as grim as a stonefish with toothache.

"You'd better get going then!" she shouted and shoved Ascott backwards. Arms flailing, he yelled and toppled off the dock. Landing with a splash in the water, he surfaced and stared up in surprised outrage. Shoal had gone, vanishing into the clapping, slapping and excitedly rapping crowd of Montabanians celebrating the arrival of the whales.

Crawling into his dugout, Ascott started the motor. Tacus waited in his position at the bow and didn't say a word as they made their way out of the log jam of boats around the dock.

Ascott fumed all the way across the shallow waters between the thousand islands of the Aardvark Archipelago. This was only the first whale pod of many that would come through the deep channel into the warm waters of the islands. There would be at least a week to see the migration and the race wouldn't happen for a day or two. He only wanted Shoal's help for one afternoon.

The canoe's outboard hummed until he was in familiar waters, then Ascott turned the boat and began tracking to where he thought Shoal had taken him fishing the day before. Opening an old metal lunchbox, he took out some crackers, a tin mug and a bottle of water.

"Bread an' water, thirty dayth!" Tacus squawked.

"More like thirty minutes. Don't fly off. I'll be back soon." The tin cup filled with water was set on the floor of the canoe, with crackers for Tacus to amuse himself with while he waited.

Ascott attached an air tank to his inflatable vest, clipped the floater on and cinched a weight belt tight around his waist. Slipping fins on his feet he positioned his goggles and took an experimental breath through the respirator. The air flowed clear and sweet into his throat. A voice in the back of his head reminded him that Shoal was right, diving alone was stupid. If you got in trouble, there would be no one to help. Another part of him coughed politely and replayed the footage of Shoal pushing him off the dock in a huff.

"Your argument is invalid," Ascott said through the respirator and toppled backwards out of the canoe.

Surfacing for a moment, he waved to Tacus and then deflated the buoyancy vest. The counter-weight of the belt dragged him down and he flicked his fins, swimming out in a search grid to find the coral-encrusted wreck.

CHAPTER 6

The search took longer than Ascott had hoped. He swam in straight lines, high enough above the bottom to see any cross-shaped masts sticking out of the sand and coral. Back and forth, crossing a wide grid that included the area he was certain Shoal had been in yesterday. The air-gauge said he had half a tank left when he found the wreck. It was invisible from most directions until you were right on top of it. Tilting his body down, Ascott kicked and swam through a school of circular plate fish, their tassel-like fins fluttering as they pushed themselves out of the way.

The wreck was half-buried in the sand and now with the air to explore at leisure, Ascott could see the boat had been holed in the port side and her spine had broken. Three shattered masts were all that remained, the sails rotted or eaten away. The ship still had the portholes for a dozen cannons on each side and now fish flitted in and out of the muzzles of the guns.

It probably sank in a hurricane. During storm season the seas became walls of white foam and the howling winds sent the trees on brief, but exhilarating, flights across the raging water.

Swimming closer, Ascott brushed away the clinging weed and a stubborn crab that clung to the gilded plank with the ship's name inscribed:

Bi . . e . . . p .

The rest was too weathered by the currents and coral to read. Ascott took a torch from his vest and clicked it on. The beam of yellow light sent the shadow fish dancing away to hide in the darkest corners as he pulled himself in through the ragged hole in the ship's wooden hull. Inside there were more fish, and silt formed from the remains of the eaten and the inedible. Ascott's movement disturbed some of the smaller creatures. The crushed bones and shells of those who hadn't hidden as well as they might have hoped moved with the silt stirred up by his fins.

Diving alone was risky; diving alone on an unknown shipwreck was an act of irresponsible lunacy. Ascott felt he had a point to prove: if there was some kind of pirate treasure here, he would be the one to find it. Shoal would have to settle for not dying on her stupid whale-running race.

And he might have enough pearls to buy a ride home sooner than the next zipillin flight.

The visibility dropped as the muck stirred up. Ascott sank deeper into the half-buried ship, pulling himself along through a particulate fog. Crabs and fish clicked and gaped at him as he slipped past, moving down a corridor that even when the ship was afloat would have been unpleasantly claustrophobic.

Some recent shift in the wreck had collapsed timbers at the end of the passage. Ascott gave one of the beams an experimental tug. It seemed wedged in tight. With a sigh of bubbles he twisted around in the tight space and found that there wasn't room for him to turn completely—the air tank jammed against the wall. Moving back slightly he tried again, twisting the other way; but the only way out was to inch backwards. Pressing his hands into the sludge on the floor he pushed and drifted. His breathing grew more rapid and the waterlogged timbers seemed to shrink in around him.

Don't think about dying, Ascott told himself.

It was hard not to keep the idea of mortality in mind. With visibility dropping to zero, he felt a growing disorientation about which way was up. He might even be going deeper into the wooden tunnel, not backing out.

Ascott screamed as something slithered over his foot. The sound was mostly inaudible, but he did manage to keep the respirator in his mouth. The slithering thing curled around his ankle and jerked him backwards. He felt a tugging on his fin and then a thrashing movement sent him spinning on to his back. Through the blizzard of silt Ascott saw that a large octopus had pulled the fin off his foot and was now trying to eat it. With a shudder, he drew his knees and remaining fin out of reach.

The octopuses of the archipelago were notoriously intelligent predators. They would eat anything and had mastered the use of simple tools to cut open shells, trap fish and, some said, to snare the occasional diver. The chance to observe one of the legendary creatures in close proximity calmed Ascott's terror. He started taking mental notes about the way the cephalopod's eight tentacles explored their surroundings as the body pulsed and shifted through a spectrum of colours.

With the octopus blocking the only exit, Ascott pulled himself along the corridor as far as the collapsed timbers. The creature turned the webbed fin over in its tentacles before casually tossing it over what passed for its shoulder. As the octopus flowed down the corridor like a bag of half-set jelly, Ascott scrambled for his dive knife, and waved the four-inch blade between himself and the octopus. The floating sack of tentacles hesitated and then all eight of its arms snapped forward. Curled in the tip of each was a variety of sharpened implements, from swords and dive knives to a fishing spear. The large unblinking eyes seemed to be saying, *Your move.*

The knife slid back into the sheath on Ascott's weight belt. He let his hands fall to the silt and mud on the floor. Watching the octopus, he felt around until a something solid passed under his fingertips. With a mental *Ah-ha!* Ascott yanked the object out of the mud and threw it at the octopus.

It was a box, flat, wooden, and about the size of a book. Its shape made it a poor choice to throw underwater, and the waterlogged case sprang open midway to its target. A set of *Ixnay* game tiles—small squares of bones with letters and smaller numbers etched into them—tumbled in suspension towards the octopus. The knives dropped and the tentacles flicked over the scattered letters, gathering them up in one eight-pronged swoop.

Ascott froze again. The octopus held each tentacle's catch of letters in front of its eyes and then with a flourish began to lay them out on the silty ground.

F-O-O-D, Ascott read. For eight points.

He shook his head and said, "I have no food." The respirator in his mouth meant it came out as "Ugh aarrgh ooh ood."

The tentacles clicked the remaining letters down in a neat pile. Moving with care, Ascott picked a sample and began to sort them and lay them out.

I-H-A-V-E-N-O-F-O-O-D. Twenty-one points. He finished with an apologetic shrug.

The octopus swept the tiles up and began to lay them out with rapid clicks. *Y-O-U-A-R-E-F-O-O-D,* seventeen points.

Ascott shook his head. The bubbles spreading along the roof of the corridor were merging into large pools that shimmered like quicksilver above his head.

The octopus gathered the tiles and laid them out again:

I-F-I-T-S-W-I-M-S-I-E-A-T-I-T. Twenty-three points and an inescapable logic.

N-O-T-F-O-O-D-S-C-I-E-N-T-I-S-T Ascott desperately spelled out. One of the octopus's tentacles curled into a large, sucker-laden *?.*

Ascott collected the letters and laid out, *N-O-T-F-O-O-D-I-N-T-E-L-L-I-G-E-N-T.* Twenty-three points, if anyone was keeping score, Ascott though.

The octopus gathered the tiles immediately and began to lay them out.

N-O-T-I-N-T-E-L-L-I-G-E-N-T-O-N-L-Y-H-A-S-T-W-O-A-R-M-S. Before Ascott could reply, the tentacles laid out a second group of tiles. F-O-R-T-Y-P-O-I-N-T-S.

Ascott gave a bubbly snort and spelled out, *T-W-O-A-R-M-S-A-N-D-B-I-G-B-R-A-I-N.* Thirty points, he mentally added.

W-H-E-R-E-B-I-G-B-R-A-I-N the octopus replied for twenty-four points.

Ascott pointed at his head. The octopus regarded him for a long moment and then laid out *O-C-T-O-P-U-S-A-L-L-B-R-A-I-N T-W-E-N-T-Y-O-N-E-P-O-I-N-T-S.*

Communicating with one of the ocean's most mysterious

creatures fascinated Ascott so much he forgot to be afraid. This appeared to be the break-through he was looking for. Finally, a sea-creature he could share information with and learn from.

Staring at the line of tiles, he calculated the scores were 133 to the octopus and 118 to Ascott.

Moving the tiles he laid out, W-E-M-A-K-E-T-H-I-N-G-S, a fair effort for twenty-five points.

The octopus responded with, Y-O-U-D-E-S-T-R-O-Y-T-H-A-W-H-I-C-H-Y-O-U-C-R-E-A-T-E. Fifty-four points. The octopus seemed intent on driving the point home and went on, M-O-R-O-N-S, for a further eight points.

Noting his air supply was getting low, Ascott laid out the letter tiles for the last time.

Y-O-U-A-R-E-R-I-G-H-T-W-E-S-H-O-U-L-D-B-E-E-A-T-E-N, forty-two points.

A braver man might have told himself that there are certainly worse ways to die than being drowned and eaten by an octopus with a killer vocabulary. Instead, Ascott found that even his eyelids were paralysed with fascination. The octopus furled its tentacles and seemed to swell in readiness to lunge in for a killing grab. Or strike. Ascott wasn't entirely sure how they did it.

The entire animal suddenly exploded in a cloud of black ink that obscured everything. In that dark cloud tentacles swirled and writhed until, in a final surge, the entire octopus vanished. Ascott blinked as several beams of light pierced the haze; he snapped off his own light and pulled himself down to the floor of the narrow corridor.

Hardly breathing, he watched while the lights played over the timbers, briefly shone into the white-out conditions of the corridor, and then vanished again. Someone else was searching the wreck.

The sound of timbers being hammered and wrenched was distorted through the water. Ascott crouched in the dark, his air gauge now touching the red. He had fifteen minutes of air left if he didn't breathe too fast. Whoever was out there seemed intent on taking the wreck apart to find whatever they were looking for. Ascott watched as his displaced fin was swept into the corridor on a stray current. Reaching out, he snatched it up and slipped it back on to his foot. Now at least he might have a swimming chance of getting out undetected.

The Ixnay box had left a clear imprint on the wooden floor where it had lain for decades before Ascott wrenched it up. He could see the locking-bolt of a trapdoor through the gap in the silt. Working the bolt free he lifted the wooden door, hoping for a chance of escape.

The space below the trapdoor was darker than the ink still clouding the water around Ascott. He hesitated, unsure whether to go in head first or risk sticking his feet in. Flicking his light back on he peered into the hole, trying to pierce the gloom. A white shape moved in the dark and then bobbed up through the gap. Ascott tumbled backwards, bubbles streaming as he yelled. The shape was a badly decayed body, the flesh hanging from the skull in white tatters. The lips were gone, giving the eyeless skull a hysterical leer. The arms were crossed over the chest, held together by the rotting coat it still wore. Clutched in the bony fingers was a metal box, similar in size and shape to the Ixnay case Ascott had wielded earlier. The skeleton rose further, twisting slowly in the current as if conducting an inspection on the state of the ship. A crab waved its claws at Ascott from her seat in the empty eye-socket, like a passenger on a skeleton-shaped zippilin.

Ascott peered into the hole until he was satisfied that this was the only dead person waiting to come up. Sliding down feet first, he snatched the metal box from the skeleton and pulled the trapdoor closed over his head. A moment later he heard the first of the other divers swim into the corridor and tug on the collapsed pile of timbers.

The water in the lower hold was clear, though completely lacking in light. His torch only emphasised the darkness as he took stock.

Seven minutes of air and no apparent way out.

Of course, the other divers might be completely harmless. It could simply be the nagging distress he suffered when faced with crowds or strangers that had driven him down here into the dark, where a dead man had been floating for Arthur-knows how long.

Now, Ascott mused, would be the perfect time for Arthur, or Drakeforth, or whatever his name actually is, to appear and perform some miracle.

Ascott didn't put a lot of faith in prayer, and he told himself this was just a fervent wish, rather than an actual appeal to a possible (retired) deity. There was no golden shaft of light, no underwater trumpet blast, and no appearance of Drakeforth. *Probably off drinking tea with Charlotte,* he thought with a pang of grief.

His grim reverie was interrupted by a tap on the shoulder, which nearly sent him through the low roof of the ship's hold in fright. Spinning around Ascott found himself face to...well, face, with the octopus. This time there were no Ixnay tiles to communicate with. The octopus spread a pair of tentacles and displayed a cut-out paper chain of human figures. A second pair of tentacles appeared with a flourish and casually ripped their paper heads off.

Seriously? Do you just sit down here waiting for people to come along so you can do this sort of thing? Ascott thought.

Looking about he saw a pointed stone lying in the mud. Snatching it up, he scraped letters in the slime-cloaked timbers: *I DON'T HAVE TIME FOR THIS.*

The octopus twirled one of its knives and scratched, *FEEDING TIME.*

NO, Ascott scratched under that. GO EAT A FISH OR SOMETHING. I HAVE TO FIND A WAY OUT OF HERE.

DON'T WANT FISH. WANT TWO ARMS NO BRAIN, the octopus wrote back.

THERE ARE MORE TWO-ARMS UP THERE, Ascott wrote, and gestured over his head for added clarity.

TWO ARMS WITH SHARP STABBY THINGS, the octopus wrote.

Great, thought Ascott. Not only is this a man-eating octopus that can read and write, it—

He became aware, with an attention-grabbing shortness of breath, that his air tank had run dry. The fat lady of panic stepped on stage to thunderous applause. Ascott flailed his arms, a thinning stream of bubbles trickling from the exit valve of his respirator.

Swimming blindly, he plunged upwards, struck his head on a low beam and stunned himself into insensibility. As consciousness hastily scrawled a note saying it didn't know what time it would be back, Ascott was only dimly aware of the arms of the octopus reaching out and gathering him up.

CHAPTER 7

Death, Ascott always assumed, would be quieter. He lay floating in a warm light, but his peaceful transition from this world to what may lie beyond the veil was being interrupted by discordant squawks and a great deal of shouting and cursing.

He opened his eyes. The sun was high in the sky and the water was an incredible shade of blue that would have interior designers throwing out their thesauruses in frustration.

"Landlubberth!" Tacus was shouting. "Thcurvy dogth!"

Ascott lifted his head to tell the bird to hush and realised that he was floating on the surface of the ocean.

His weight belt and air-tank were gone, but on the plus side, he hadn't been eaten by an octopus. Moving his feet and hands so he floated upright, Ascott took stock. A large cruiser boat drifted less than a hundred feet away, shining with a blue and white glossy finish. It was one of those rich-man motor yachts, all sleek lines and wooden panelling inside.

Tacus was at the end of his rope, literally and figuratively. His wings flapped as he strained against a cord that was tied around his feet, preventing him from escaping more than a few feet from the deck of the cruiser.

Ascott turned slowly, putting together a complete picture of what was happening. *Tacus is being kidnapped by rich people; my dive gear is gone; and my canoe is on fire.*

That required a second look. The dugout was indeed ablaze, and had burned down to the water line already. A column of thick black smoke rose into the clear sky.

Ascott started swimming towards the cruiser. A small part of his mind, the part that wasn't prepared to draw conclusions based on mere observation, thought that they might have, at best, a fire-extinguisher; and at worst, an explanation.

Kalim Aari appeared on deck and turned his sunglasses towards Ascott.

"My canoe is on fire!" Ascott called up to him.

"Yes, yes it is," Kalim replied as if Ascott had commented on the pleasantness of the weather.

"My *canoe* is on *fire!*" Ascott repeated.

"I know! I set it on fire!" Kalim called back.

"Why would you do that!?" Ascott treaded water as he yelled.

"Because you are more likely to cooperate if you are in danger of drowning!"

"I've been in danger of drowning once already today! It didn't make me cooperative at all!"

"Mutiny!" Tacus squawked as he landed heavily on the deck and began to pick at the rope around his legs.

Kalim leaned on the chrome rail of the boat, "Where is it?" he said to Ascott.

"Where is what?" Ascott cast about, looking for whatever it might be that Kalim had mislaid.

"The treasure."

"What treasure?"

"My uncle was Captain Tithely Aarrgh. His grand-father, Fencer Aarrgh, was the first Captain Aarrgh. Fencer Aarrgh buried a great treasure somewhere on these islands and wrote the secret to its location in a logbook that he kept in an iron box. His ship, the *Bilgepuppy*, went down in a hurricane two days later. Captain Aarrgh was never seen or heard from again." Kalim moved along the rail to keep up with Ascott, who was swimming towards the back of the boat.

"How do you know he found the treasure and wrote the secret down in a log book and put that in a metal box if he went down with his ship two days later?" Ascott asked as he edged towards the rear of the boat.

Kalim ignored the question. "They say my uncle found the

treasure, but went mad. I don't think that is true. I think he never found the treasure and went mad anyway."

"Not finding a treasure that may not exist would drive you crazy," Ascott agreed. He reached the dive platform on the back of the cruiser and started to pull himself up. Kalim levelled a loaded spear-gun at his face.

"I've had people dive the wreck of my great-granduncle's ship, and they can't find anything. You were diving around here. I think you might have found it."

"I found an old ship. I don't know about any treasure, I'm just here to research the fish."

Kalim frowned. "What fish?"

"All the fish, any fish. The fish of the Aardvark Archipelago," Ascott found it increasingly irritating that no one appreciated the task he had taken upon himself.

"Why do you want to do that?" Kalim asked, the spear-gun aiming steadily at Ascott's right eye.

"Because there are thousands of unique species of marine life in these islands. No one has ever seen them before."

"Did you lose a bet or something?" Kalim asked.

"No. I'm writing the definitive encyclopaedia about the fish of these islands, and—why does everyone find that so funny?!" he snapped as Kalim went from merely grinning to actively chuckling.

"You seriously think that anyone cares about a bunch of fish?"

"I care!" Ascott shouted. "These islands are a unique environment, the shallow waters and coral reefs give a perfect isolated breeding ground for species not found anywhere else in the world!"

"How do you know? Have you been everywhere in the world? Have you seen every fish there is?"

Ascott gaped up at Kalim. "Now you're just being ridiculous," he said.

"I've travelled all over. I've dived wrecks, reefs, ridges, and whirlpools. I've seen more fish than I can count, and you know the one thing that I've always noticed about them?"

Ascott shook his head.

"They all look the same! Now get your hands off my boat, unless you can tell me where the treasure is."

Ascott let go of the ladder and sank back into the water. "I don't know anything about any treasure."

Kalim turned his head and shouted an order to someone at the helm. "As soon as the divers are back on board, we're heading out!"

The water around Ascott bubbled and churned; he swam backwards and a moment later two divers surfaced at the back of the cruiser. They barely gave him a glance as they stripped their tanks and weight belts, passing them up to a deck hand who stowed the gear and helped the divers aboard.

Kalim appeared at the back of the boat again, the spear gun over his shoulder at a jaunty angle. He grinned and waved to Ascott as the boat engines coughed into life and it began to pull away.

"You can't just leave me here!" Ascott yelled, waving his arms. Kalim waved back and the boat picked up speed, leaving Ascott adrift in a sea of choppy foam. The sound of Tacus accusing his kidnappers of an unhealthy interest in animal husbandry was the last thing to fade as the boat shrank towards the horizon.

The remains of the canoe eventually fizzled out like a wet fire-cracker. Steam and smoke drifted from the scorched log as Ascott calculated the minimum distance he would have to swim to reach anywhere. He figured he had as much chance of making it as he did of setting the steaming remains of the canoe on fire again to keep warm.

With nothing else to do before slipping exhausted beneath the waves, Ascott pondered the larger situation. Charlotte was still alive, but Drakeforth had said there was nothing that could be done to change what was already happening. A sense of powerlessness washed over him, and for the first time since childhood Ascott found himself crying. A weeping tantrum of frustration against the implacable and unknowable nature of the Universe. If the Arthurians were right—and even Drakeforth gave them some credit—humanity was a long way from understanding anything about the true nature of most of the inexhaustibly confusing things that made up the dimensions of space and time that they blunder about in.

"Is it any wonder," Drakeforth had said over blood-flavoured tea, "that people believe in things like religion?"

"I don't need religion," Ascott said aloud to the blistering afternoon sun. "I just need to know that my life means something. That when I am gone, I have done something to contribute to the collective knowledge of the world. Why is that so hard for people to accept? But no one cares about fish, do they? No, it's all treasure and saving the world and not telling your only surviving family that you are *dying*!" He slapped the water in frustration and thought about just letting himself sink.

Even if he got a ticket and the zipillin flew out of Montaban in time, what could he do? It was always Charlotte who managed social occasions and talked to strangers with ease. When Ascott left, she was working in her chosen field of computer psychology. It seemed in the here and now that even if he went charging home to save her, Charlotte would tell him that he wasn't needed. She would take care of things, because that was what Charlotte did.

My entire contribution to society has been —what? A poor excuse for a brother, a half-finished book that no one else believes in, a foster-parent to a mad-parrot, and a joke to the people of Montaban.

With a quiet *bloop*, the metal box he had snatched from the dead man's grasp surfaced next to him. Ascott stared at it, and then ducked his head under to see where it came from. Far below, he could just make out the fluid shape of a large octopus picking its way over the coral and sand.

Oh, very funny, he thought. His entry on the giant octopus of the archipelago was going to include a reference to them being the most irritating of the invertebrates.

As the sun sank lower in the sky thirst came and Ascott smiled grimly through cracked lips. Up to his neck in water, and he seemed doomed to die of dehydration. The same way that one of the Aarrghs had gone. Was it the first or the second Aarrgh? He couldn't quite remember. It probably wasn't important. One of them found a treasure, or didn't. Then the second one found the same treasure, or didn't either. It made no sense. Why would two people find a treasure only for one to get sunk in a hurricane and the other one to go mad? Ascott wanted to ask the octopus why the sky and the sea were the same blue. Surely it meant that the fish were at risk of swimming up into the stratosphere?

Density, the octopus typed on the same old Klang Mk II mechanical typewriter that Ascott used for writing up his research. Fresh water has a density of 1 gram per cubic centimetre. The human body has an average density of 1.062 grams per cubic centimetre. Sea water has a density of 1.025 and the sun has a density of 1.40 grams per cubic centimetre. The sun is made up of hydrogen and helium...

Ascott stopped listening. The rapid clicking of the typewriter keys sounded like an orchestra of tone deaf crabs playing the castanets. "Quiet," he muttered, thrashing his arms and tasting fresh salt on his lips. "I have infinite density," he mumbled as the waves washed over his face like an incoming tide.

CHAPTER 8

Shoal was not one to hold a grudge. She tended to resolve any problems before they had time to become grudges. At age six, while out fishing with her year group in what passed for school in Montaban, Charlie Meninges had put fish guts in her hair. In response she punched him so hard his nose bled.

She didn't advocate violence, although she did have a rock solid belief in not letting people get away with making your plaits stink of fish guts for the rest of the day. Her fight with Ascott bothered her. Pushing him in the water had been stupid. She wasn't going to apologise, but maybe they could share a pizza and she would listen while he talked about the latest fish that he had "discovered."

The skiff bounced from wave to wave; she rode the turbulence with the casual grace of an experienced equestrian. (Shoal had never seen a horse, except in pictures; they were odd-looking things with big teeth and she wasn't convinced they were real.)

A dark smudge on the horizon caught her attention. It was out of place, like a fly floating in a glass of milknut juice. Watching the hazy cloud, she absently patted the outboard motor and encouraged it to go faster. The spray stung like tears on her cheeks and the skiff slammed through the low swells. The smudge resolved into a drifting pillar of smoke, slowly dissipating in the still air; in another hour the sky would be dark and the smoke invisible. Smoke on the water usually meant trouble, but fire in the sky would be worse. Shoal slowed the boat as she reached the source, a single charred log floating just under the surface.

She wondered how it ended up out here.

Turning the engine off, she let the boat drift, scanning the water for any signs or explanation. A faint voice floated across the water.

"While the Fophler fish appears to be similar in shape and colouring to the Phofler fish, differences can be noted in the dorsal fin shape and mating habits. The Fophler favours one-night stands after which the male actively avoids contact with the female, while the Phofler tends to mate for life, or until one of the pair gets eaten by a predator…"

"City boy?" Shoal called across the water. "Where are you?" Using a paddle she pushed the boat forward until she saw Ascott's head bobbing above the waves. His head rolled and he waved weakly to his invisible audience with one hand.

"It's bigger than just fish," he announced. Shoal stowed the paddle and reached out to pull Ascott on board. A dark purple shape swelled and then contracted under the water. As she heaved Ascott's limp form up, a giant octopus released him and shot away into deeper water.

"It's everything…" Ascott muttered. "That's what drives you mad."

"You drive me mad," Shoal said, opening Ascott's mouth with one hand and trickling fresh water from a milknut bottle onto his half-baked tongue. "Always going off and getting into trouble. That's twice this week I've had to save you." She stared at his sun-blistered face with gentle concern. Ascott's earnest fascination with fish seemed harmless until he got himself in trouble like this. She gave him more water, and he seemed to slip into a doze, one arm clutched protectively around an old metal box. Shoal started the boat, turning towards the island where Ascott lived with Tacus, and wondered why her mother saw marriage potential in the strange boy from the city.

The white sand glowed under the moonlight. As the skiff ran up the beach and the engine sighed and relaxed, Ascott opened his eyes.

"Shoal," he croaked.

"Hey, city boy," she said.

"They took Tacus." Ascott sat up, and winced, a hand going to his head. "They kidnapped him."

"Who?" Shoal scowled in a way that Charlie Meninges would have recognised.

"Pirates," Ascott said. Shoal let her scowl relax.

"There are no pirates, not anymore."

"Yes there are. They drive big cruiser motor yachts and are looking for treasure. That wreck we found—they think that it holds a secret. Probably in this box. They were looking for it, but the octopus took it away and then we played Ixnay."

"You were floating out there for hours. The sun and thirst can make you see strange things," Shoal said.

"The octopus…it wanted to eat me, but then it came up and kept me afloat. I remember trying to explain to it about the fish. Drakeforth told me that fish aren't the important thing. It is bigger than fish."

"What is?" Shoal stepped out of the boat and helped Ascott step on to the sand.

"I don't know. Maybe the treasure? But treasure isn't every-thing. Is it?"

"It could be, to some people. You need to get some rest, and stay out of the sun," Shoal guided him up the beach and into the cool interior of his bamboo hut. She laid him down on his bed and got a glass of fresh water from the tap that connected to the desalination tank humming away outside.

"Drink this," she ordered and he did so, draining the glass and gasping as he lay down again. "Now get some sleep," she said, but Ascott was already unconscious.

CHAPTER 9

While Ascott slept, Shoal tidied up. The open suitcase made her frown. Ascott had said something about going back to The City. It seemed he was serious.

There wasn't much for her to do. A few pizza boxes to bundle up for return to Montaban, sweep the sand outside, and Tacus' drawings to tidy away. She regarded a sample critically. Most of the pictures were the same: an outline in green or blue, with squiggles and lines inside the shape. She rifled through them, stacking one page on the next, noticing that each picture was a repeat of the last. Shoal wondered what could obsess the parrot so much. Ascott said they were amoebas, which he claimed were tiny living blobs that lived in water, which you couldn't see without using a microscope. A device, she thought, that sounded as fanciful as a horse. Besides, how would a parrot know what an amoeba looked like? The only amoeba she knew of was the island of Saint Amoeba, named after one of the Arthurian missionaries who arrived in the islands two hundred years ago. It was considered sacred now. Visiting the island was forbidden, unless you were a bird or a turtle or a competitor in the annual whale migration race.

The race started on the tiny rock known as Arthur's Nose and went across the channel to the beach of Saint Amoeba. South of Amoeba and the Nose the channel got deeper, and this was the only way in or out of the archipelago at low tide. Especially if you were a pod of whales, or a ship with a keel.

After sunset the temperature dropped from baking to merely

warm, so Shoal put on one of Ascott's shirts and sat on the porch watching the moon and the waves. She couldn't imagine living anywhere but on the islands. She had been born on Montaban and had explored every inch of the myriad channels between the islands since she was old enough to handle a boat on her own, which coincidentally was when she was old enough to punch boys like Charlie Meninges in the face.

It was peaceful sitting in the moonlight, listening to the heartbeat of the ocean, the gentle pulse of the waves whispering to the sand. To Shoal the water was a living thing, a vast creature that breathed and moved. She felt as close to it as she did her own family. When she was small, Sandy had told her how people came from the sea and they were still mostly sea water.

"To the sea we return," he said. It was the day they buried Nana Smith, Sandy's mother. The old lady had been laid to rest in the traditional way. A service was held in the Exco's Arthurian chapel and then her body was taken out on a boat. With family present, the old woman's body was gently floated into the water, and the currents took her away.

Shoal preferred to be in the water than on land. The idea of being away from the sight, sound and smell of the sea was something she could not comprehend. She knew that for most people the sea was a strange and fearful place, but for her it was like a return to the womb.

Shoal stood up. The house was still and quiet; Ascott was asleep and the waves stirred the sand. She walked down to the water, shedding her clothes until, naked, she walked into the waves and dived. The warm water flowed over her skin, making her feel streamlined and fleet as a fish.

The world under the waves was entirely silent, buoyant and still. The gentle push of currents and tidal shifts was easy to ride and they carried her to the edge of the lagoon in one record-beating breath. She broke the surface with barely a ripple and exhaled slowly. Taking in her next lungful of air she dived down again. Her body cutting through the water, she passed beyond the reef and into the stronger currents that flowed like coiling rivers around the islands.

The sea shaped the land as much as the land shaped the sea. The ancient rock lay mostly below the water, keeping it shallow and warm enough for life to get really crazy. The colder deep-sea mixing with the warm surface water carried food through an infinite cycle of wash; where eggs, smelt, or spores found purchase on the rocks, life took hold.

The channel was the only way to leave the archipelago by sea; everywhere else was too shallow for big boats. With Montaban being the biggest island, it made sense that people lived there and it certainly made borrowing a cup of milknut crumbs from your neighbours more convenient.

Shoal stopped swimming and let the water carry her. The occasional colder current raised goose bumps on her skin and made the return to warmer thermoclines more pleasant. After eight minutes underwater even Shoal's lungs burned, so she rose to the surface and floated on her back, catching her breath under the stars.

The islands existed as a living body. Everything in the water or on the rocks was part of that living, breathing entity. Shoal knew this with a deep awareness that she could not describe; it would be like asking fish to define water.

Only Ascott was an enigma, even for a boy from the city. He loved the ocean in a different way. Not content to simply be a part of it, he needed to take it apart, see why it resonated with him and somehow understand it in a context that he could put in something as flat and dull as a book. To begin with Shoal had thought he was just odd, and in true Montaban fashion she had taken care of him—the same way one would take care of a seabird that had been blown in by a hurricane.

Like a stormed gull, without help he would not have survived. He couldn't feed himself, or find shelter or run a boat. She had taught him as much as she could. The pizzas were a source of amusement to everyone who knew about them. That crazy city fella, sitting in the middle of the biggest larder in the world and he insists on eating frozen stuff shipped in from The City, they said. *City people eh?* they would say and nod over their mugs of java.

She'd never defended him aloud, never told the people who sat around the bars laughing at him to shut their faces. She'd just taken care of him, bringing him his weird food, telling him that it was being charged on his credit stick. Not that anyone on Montaban had much use for credit sticks. Pearls and favours were the common currency. Shoal did some fishing and boat cleaning each week for Old Sam, the teller at the Exco who ordered pizzas in bulk and stacked them up in the big freezer out the back.

"So what is he doing for you?" the grey-haired old-timer had asked her one time when she made her regular pick up.

"Nothing. He's just here to look at the fish," she replied, unable to meet the old man's eye.

"Reckon you've gone soft for him, eh?" The clerk's eyes gleamed with good-natured humour. Shoal shrugged and hurried out of the Exco with the loaded chiller box in her arms.

Just because she liked him, didn't mean she had to marry him. Her mother was annoying, always asking after Ascott. Asking why Shoal didn't invite him home for a meal.

"He's too skinny that boy. How can he be a good provider if he's that skinny?" she would wail.

"Mum," Shoal would reply. "Just leave it."

Ascott could swim all right and he could catch all the fish he wanted. He just chose not to. Shoal didn't mind that Ascott only cared about the fish. And she'd always known that when he had written about all the fish he thought no one knew about simply because he had never seen them before, he would go back to his home. But now he was preparing to leave early.

Shoal couldn't imagine leaving the archipelago; she would die like a beached fish in The City.

CHAPTER 10

Ascott woke up to the sound of Tacus squawking. He lay there a moment, thinking about the pros and cons of teaching the parrot to get his own biscuits from the cupboard. The mess would be horrendous, but it might be worth it for a few more minutes of undisturbed sleep in the mornings.

It was no good, he was awake now. Opening his eyes Ascott sat up, put his feet on the wooden floor and reached for a shirt. Walking out to the kitchen he boiled water for tea and went to the window overlooking the veranda and the beach beyond.

Tacus wasn't at his usual place on the table. Shoal was sitting there instead, her head on her folded arms, asleep. Ascott stood in the window, regarding the view. Shoal was wearing one of his shirts and her usual cut-off shorts. The light morning breeze stirred her short hair and her sleeping face was the most serene he had ever seen her. Ascott wondered what it would be like to know that kind of peace.

"What?" Shoal murmured, her eyes still closed.

"What?" Ascott replied with a guilty start.

"You're staring at me," Shoal said, and began to move with great reluctance as if the chair and table where the most comfortable bed imaginable. Her eyes opened, and she stretched. Ascott went to make the tea.

The gulls screeching overhead sounded like Tacus, from a distance.

"How will we find him?" Ascott said and stirred the leaves in the bottom of his empty cup.

"There's only one way out of the islands for a boat of that size, and that's going to be blocked off by whales for the next week."

"We don't even know if they are trying to leave. Everything Kalim said suggests they are looking for something here in the islands."

"Buried treasure?" Shoal gave a snort. "People are always looking for buried treasure. It's one of the main reasons city folk come out here."

"They ever find any?" Ascott thought that a chest full of loot might solve a lot of problems right now.

"There was this one fella, Skimpy Gherkin, he made treasure maps. He would draw them, stain them with tea and then leave them in the sun for a few days. Then he would send them off to some city fella who would leave them in old books and things for people to find. The maps had enough information on them to guide who ever found it to Montaban. After that he would lay out a random bunch of clues like, *Twenty paces from the shark's tooth and dig under the sign of the red moon.*"

"Did anyone fall for it?"

"Quite a few people, yeah. There were some seasons when we had whole groups of city people turning up with shovels and asking strange questions about local landmarks."

"That's kind of cruel," Ascott suggested.

"Montaban did well out of the tourism for a while. No one took it seriously until one of the maps turned out to lead to actual buried treasure."

"You're kidding?" Ascott set down his cup and stared at Shoal.

"True as, eh. A small chest of gold coins that dated back to the olden days when ships would stop over here. Worth quite a bit nowadays. Bound to happen sooner or later, I guess. Lots of old wrecks in these islands. Someone must have buried treasure somewhere."

"Skimpy must have buried the treasure to get more people to come to the islands."

"Nope, Skimpy swore till he was blue that he had no idea where the coins came from. Said his maps were all a joke to get tourists to visit. Didn't stop people looking, though. The city fella heard about the treasure they'd found and rounded up all the maps Skimpy'd been making to search for himself. Plenty of other city folk searched, but they never found much."

"Did the man from The City find any treasure?"

Shoal shrugged. "No—he took to calling himself Captain Aarrgh and went crazy. The Seaguard went to find him after he started attacking other sailors and they ended up bringing his boat in. They reckon he drowned."

"Your mum and dad told me about Captain Aarrgh. They reckon he went mad because he found treasure."

"Maybe." Shoal frowned, "What kind of treasure would drive you crazy?"

"Maybe there was a trap, some kind of poison that made him go insane?"

"Never heard that theory before." Shoal finished her tea and started to clear the dishes. "Whale races will be starting today, you going to come and watch?"

Ascott hesitated. The idea of being in the tight press of spectators made his skin crawl, and he desperately wanted to start the search for the blue cruiser and rescue Tacus.

But the thought of abandoning Shoal as she risked her life for a driftwood trophy didn't appeal, either.

"Sure," he heard himself saying. "I'll be there to cheer you on." Shoal's answering smile was brighter than the morning sun sparkling on the water.

"After I win, we can go looking for that boat and get Tacus back," she said. Ascott nodded and then froze as Shoal kissed him on the cheek before vanishing inside with the breakfast dishes.

On rubbery legs, Ascott retrieved the metal box from his room. The sea had sealed it shut with rust and coral. A few sharp blows with a rock sheared the crusted latch off.

"If it's not water-tight, whatever was inside will be ruined," Ascott said.

"Only one way to find out." Shoal leaned over the table on her elbows, her face alight with curiosity.

The box squealed and resisted when Ascott pulled on the lid.

He took a better grip and strained harder. With a final scream of protest the corroded hinges broke and the container sprang open. A bundle wrapped in dark leather and tied with a cord thudded out on the table.

"Fruity," Shoal said. Ascott nodded. Other than the bundle, the small box was empty. He put it aside and began to work on unknotting the leather cord.

"Here, let me, I'm good with knots."

Ascott sat back as Shoal pulled a knife and slashed through the leather string with one quick strike.

"What?" she asked as Ascott shook his head. Unwrapping the leather shroud revealed a small book. It looked old, but more importantly, it seemed to be dry. Ascott gently opened its leather-bound cover and slowly read the faded ink aloud. "The Log an' Jyrnl of Fensa Aarrgh. Capn o' the Bilgepuppy."

"Fencer Aarrgh—he was a real pirate. Is there a treasure map in there?" Shoal moved around the table to stare more closely at the faded text while Ascott turned the pages.

"Jany fit'teen. Caught a merchant sloop boun' for Montaban. Nothin' on "er cept a brace of hairy fellas. Crew's spirits lifted when they fig'ud that some of the hairy fella's were wimmin in disguys. No loot." Ascott turned more pages, "Jany sick'teen, Calm, no ships. Jany sen'teen, Calm, used upwind whale for cannon target practice, blubba all over deck and drippin' off sales. Jany hate'teen, Light breeze, Can still smell whale. Doc reckons could use whale spit to make soap and perfoom. Had Doc flogged for ~~insuboar, insoboo~~ for bein' looney."

"Why would you want to make soap and perfume from whale spit?" Shoal wrinkled her nose.

"Well, it's not like you can eat them," Ascott suggested.

"Certainly not a whole one," Shoal agreed.

"Jany twentieth, nothing...Jany twen'one, Cookie boiled up whale bits, whole crew got the runs, Doc still recovrin from floggin'. Havin' to give orders from stern seat o'er the rail. Jany twen'too, have promised double share of next lootin' to any man who can find me soft paper."

"Oh for a life at sea," Shoal said. Ascott smiled and flicked through more pages.

"Here's something. January twenty-fourth. My name is Dentine Tubule, ship's surgeon. I have taken command of the *Bilgepuppy* after the captain and crew were stricken with food-poisoning. I know little of seamanship and cannot raise the sails unaided. The sky is dark with an approaching storm. I am steering with the currents as best I can for the nearest jungle-clad isle. I pray to Arthur and all his saints that I can ground the ship before the tempest arrives."

Ascott turned the page. "January twenty-sixth. Fate has brought us to our goal on the wings of a storm that battered us terribly. But we are safe ensconced in a cove on an unexplored island, one of many in the Aardvark Archipelago. The captain has roused himself and his ghastly crew. He intends for us to go ashore, seeking soft leaves and, perhaps, an Arthurian missionary settlement to sack. Given the crew's current state of unstable health, I am to accompany them. Luckily the captain has shown no interest in updating the ship's log, so it falls to me to remain the scribe of our miserable adventure…

> *January 27th.*
>
> *My hands shake as I recall the events of the last two days. I am sure it is only two, as we have seen the moon fly over us but twice. Of this I am sure. There is a madness that nips at my heels like a small dog. I claim the right to be mad; indeed much of the crew have succumbed and have run off into the undergrowth shrieking and rolling in the dirt. Only the captain has remained steadfast. Perhaps it is his lack of imagination — or wits — that has prevented him from attempting to understand what we have witnessed. Understanding shall be my downfall.*
>
> *My captain and crew are pirates. I fear the adventurous notion of such a career that I fostered as a child is far from the reality. They are a bunch of brutal, callous men, with the collective intellect of a plate of cucumber sandwiches. It tests my faith to realise that the forces of the Universe have deemed that they alone be the discoverers of a treasure beyond imagining.*

The captain is making ready to return to that hidden place, so un-artfully discovered, and make the treasure his own. I fear he lacks the number of stout men required to lift that much gold.

I will have no part to play in this. Instead I shall hide myself and this log in the lower hold and pray that when we make landfall at the fishing village of Montaban I will be able to escape and warn the world.

If this log is found, know that these are not my last words. I shall continue to record my misadventure in an invisible hand.

Ascott turned the page and then more, right through to the back cover, but all the remaining pages were blank.

"So it wasn't the captain's body you found in the wreck?" Shoal shivered. "That poor doctor. It's a horrible way to die."

"I was hoping it would tell us what happened, why the ship sank and what became of the crew." Ascott put the antique book down and frowned at it.

"We can go through it again later. If we don't get moving we won't be there for the start of the race. We can report Tacus' kidnapping to the Seaguard, too."

Ascott returned the log book to the box and put the container under his bed. Heading out, he caught up with Shoal at the water's edge as she pushed her boat out.

CHAPTER 11

The port of Montaban was more crowded than usual. The fishing fleet was home for the races, the docks and streets were draped in colourful streamers, and hot air balloons made of paper in the shape of whales were drifting out over the bay.

"Is it always like this?" Ascott asked as they merged with the boat traffic buzzing around the docks.

"Migration comes but once a year!" Shoal grinned.

Music and laughter echoed across the water, everywhere people danced and waved ribbons and flags. Bands of musicians blew haunting notes through shells, strummed guitars and pounded milknut drums in a cacophony of joyous revelry. The java flowed freely and even the stall holders had paused in their relentless sales pitch to join in the festivities.

"What about the Seaguard? We need to tell them about Tacus." Ascott squeezed through the gyrating crowd after Shoal, who forded the mass of people as easily as wading through breakers.

"No time! They'll be busy today anyway!" Shoal's hand came back and grabbed Ascott's, pulling him after her as she pushed through the dancers and started running up the narrow street towards Smith's Dive Emporium.

Ascott caught his breath in the cool shade inside the shop. Shoal vanished upstairs, shouting something about getting changed and being right back.

Standing around waiting for her, Ascott saw the mural under the waveboards again. He took a closer look. The seated figure, laughing heartily from within a circle of milknut trees, completely dwarfed a group of tiny figures who danced in front of him. *Weird,* Ascott thought. Arthurianism was the official religion of the islands, but Ascott saw signs of an older belief system everywhere. Carved statues, faded murals showing giant fish, pendants that represented sea-spirits and gods of storms. So who was the laughing giant?

"Come on!" Shoal dashed past in a figure-hugging one-piece body suit that came half-way down her arms and thighs. Ascott ran after her.

This time when they ran into the revelling crowd a roar of adulation went up and the people parted, waving and cheering as they made way for Shoal in her racing costume. Ascott followed close in her wake, running in the tight vacuum before the crowd swelled closed again.

They ran on to the dock and the crowd roared louder. Shoal swung down a ladder and landed on a powered barge where other similarly dressed competitors stood waiting. Ascott scrambled down and took his place next to her.

"Hey, competitors only, man," said a young guy wearing a t-shirt with *OFISHAL* printed on the front.

"Back off Charlie, he's with me," Shoal warned.

Charlie paled visibly and stepped back. "Okay, Shoal, okay."

Somewhere a horn sounded, the crowd roared and surged towards their boats. The barge's engines hummed into life and they made their way out of the port.

"I will now read the rules of the 367th Annual Montaban Whale Race!" Charlie called over the noise of the crowd and the boats zipping around them. "Only authorised competitors can enter the course. To successfully complete the crossing each competitor must traverse the channel on the back of migrating whales. Any attempt to use artificial locomotion will result in disqualification. Ten points will be deducted for every minute you are in the water. Competitors will wear officially ordained whale-running shoes. Bare feet and other forms of footwear are forbidden to be worn during each race. There will be a thirty-minute delay for judges' deliberation between each race. The top three runners from each of the three rounds will compete in a final crossing to determine the overall winner. Try not to get killed."

A few of the competitors cheered and clapped; most, including Shoal, just stared at the horizon, faces tight with determination.

"Shoal," Ascott whispered. "You could die doing this. It's not too late to back out."

She turned and looked at him, as if noticing his presence for the first time. "On average eight out of thirty competitors are injured each year. Of that eight, three die, usually by drowning or from crush injuries. There have only been two instances of shark attack in the recorded history of the race. In both cases the competitor survived. A woman has only been champion nineteen times in the last three hundred and sixty-seven years. Anything else you think I don't know?"

"Uhh...the Southern Rong Whale travels in pods of up to forty-five individuals. A mix of males and females. They will be on the surface because of the shallow beam of the channel at the crossing point. Your best option is to get on at the caudal peduncle, that's the bit on the back right before the tail, and then quickly move up the dorsal ridge. Position yourself forward of the dorsal fin. Then time your jump to the next whale just after it's blown. Again, aim for the base of the tail. See if you can catch the dorsal ridge and watch out for roll-over and other runners."

Shoal nodded at him. "Thanks, Coach."

"Other than that, run. Don't stop, don't hesitate and don't look at what anyone else is doing."

She nodded, and began to stretch, bending her knees and flexing her arms. She took a traditional pair of whale-running shoes from her bag and strapped them on. The shoes reminded Ascott of a weird cross between snowshoes and sandals. Made from woven milknut fibre, their wide soles and the rough material provided grip on the slick skin of a surging behemoth.

He stepped back and waited in grim silence until the boat reached the tiny island of Arthur's Nose. The channel was at its narrowest here and while the water was just deep enough for keeled ships to go on to the port at Montaban, the southern tip of the Nose marked the drop off point into deeper water.

Small craft already jostled for position around the island. The rock itself, which would have been standing room only for more than a couple of people, was packed with expectant spectators.

"Competitors in round one, take your positions!" Charlie yelled. Shoal squeezed Ascott's hand and stepped up to the edge of the barge, facing the channel.

"Good luck!" Ascott called and felt immediately self-conscious. Shoal didn't look back. Her focus was on the surging water where large grey shapes rose and fell, sending spray jetting into the air from their blowholes and the massive slaps of their tail flukes on the surface.

A shell horn trumpeted the start of the race. Shoal and eleven other competitors dove off the edge of the barge. The water churned with their passage. Ascott shaded his eyes and watched a blonde head break the surface a good body-length in front of the rest of the field. Swimming strongly, Shoal aimed for the thickest clump of whales. They were also moving, swimming in an almost playfully casual way after their long journey from the cold, dark waters of the southern ocean.

This was the Rong whales' summer vacation, their chance to wallow in warm, shallow waters and welcome the next generation into the world. They would spend a few weeks here to let the newborns find their fins before beginning the long journey back to the rich feeding grounds under the southern icepack.

No boats were allowed through the channel during the migration, partly because there was a chance of injury to the whales, but mostly because there was a far greater chance of your boat being smashed to pieces by a sea-creature weighing in excess of a hundred tonnes.

Charlie had binoculars trained on the swimmers, who were already vanishing into the churning water around the pod. Nearby, judges stood in boats and observed through their own spyglasses.

"Shoal's on the first whale, scoring begins," Charlie announced. Ascott squinted into the glare of the sun. He could see nothing now, just foam and the reflection from the whales as they surfaced, blew water and air, and then dived again.

A sudden chorus of *"Oooohh!"* came from the spectators with telescopic eyewear.

"What happened?" Ascott demanded.

"Serro slipped, he'll lose points for being in the water," Charlie replied without taking his eyes off the race.

"Where's Shoal Smith?"

"Still in the lead, closely followed by Nonkin, Timmlin is in third place. Smith's on her second whale, a bull by the size of him, she's going to have to get some height to make it to—*OOH!*"

Ascott nearly exploded in desperate frustration. "What!?"

"Nonkin collided with Smith—she's hanging on to the dorsal ridge with one hand, trying to get her feet up. If she can stay out of the water, she won't lose points." Charlie spoke faster and louder. The next round's competitors were hanging on to every word and someone started offering three to one odds that Timmlin would come from behind and win.

"Smith's back up, Nonkin's made the transfer to the next whale, Smith is running up to the head! She's going to try and jump! She's—she's—she's made it! Shoal is in the lead!" Charlie jumped up and down waving his arms. Ascott snatched the binoculars and focused them on the race.

"Come on, Shoal," he muttered. He tensed, watching the distant shape leap from whale to whale, clambering up the curved spine of the dorsal ridge and throwing herself across the gap to the next whale.

"What's happening, man!?" Charlie tried to pull the binoculars from Ascott, who jerked back. "Shoal is still in the lead, but I think that's Nonkin coming up fast. Oh! That can't be legal! He tripped her! Shoal is down! She's in the water!"

Ascott lowered the glasses and stared in horror at the distant scene. Raising the binoculars again he focused in on the spot where Shoal had disappeared. "Timmlin and the rest of the pack are catching up. If she doesn't get up soon she'll lose too many points!"

"Remember, competitors lose ten points for every minute they are in the water," Charlie announced.

"There she goes! Oh, she looks mad!" Ascott danced from

foot to foot. "There's only a few hundred yards left! Nonkin's on the next whale! Shoal is two behind him! Timmlin is hot on her heels! The rest of the field are having trouble!"

"Anyone down?" Charlie asked.

"Uh…I can only see three people behind Timmlin. I guess the rest are swimming it. A green flag just went up on the beach! What does that mean?"

"Green flag!" Charlie yelled, "Nonkin wins the first round!"

"Come on Shoal…Black flag! That's Shoal, right?" Ascott turned to Charlie.

"Black flag! Smith takes second place!"

"Red flag!" someone else yelled. "Timmlin is third!"

The official result came back that Beval Nonkin had won the race by coming in first. Shoal's silver position was threatened by the points deducted for her time in the water, but she still managed to beat Syreus Timmlin by twenty-five points to take second. The three of them would be going through to the final race, which was scheduled for that evening.

Ascott paced up and down, waiting for the finalists to be brought back to starting line. He didn't watch the second heats, in which last year's champion, Lody Fashbean, had to be pulled from the water with a gashed scalp and concussion after he fell and took a fluke slap to the head.

The third race was the lowest scoring, as there was a lull in whales even after the start was delayed for several hours. Denio Vanya won, which meant that she and Shoal were the only two women competing in the final.

Medical boats ferried over a dozen injured back to Montaban, though by the time the third race was decided no fatalities had been reported for the day and the party was in full swing from Montaban to the Nose.

Ascott stopped pacing as the waiting crowd roared at the twilight, welcoming the crowded boat carrying the nine finalists as it chugged in to port. Getting close to Shoal was challenging. The press of people wanting to offer congratulations to the winners made it impossible for him to get within reach.

"Ascott!" Shoal yelled over the heads of the crowd.

"Shoal! I'm here!" Ascott waved and plunged into the hot mass of people. The close smell of them, the raucous shouts of their voices and the press of their skin almost made him gag. He kept going, finally breaking through the ring of people around Shoal.

"You came second!" he grinned.

Shoal hugged him. "One more race to go!" she howled and the crowd cheered with her.

"Attention, competitors in the final race!" Charlie had a megaphone now and his voice echoed across the water and muted the crowd. "The final race will be going ahead. Competitors are advised to exercise extreme caution as it is likely to be dark before the race is completed. Race will begin in fifteen minutes! Competitors to the race barge!"

The crowd parted and many moved off to find a good position to see the race. The setting sun gave way to the rising moon that illuminated the scene in a high-contrast white glow. Ascott took his place once again on the competitors' barge and tried to look like he was meant to be there. The officials and finalists waited as the reports came in that several pods of whales were moving in to the channel. The various self-proclaimed experts agreed that this would mean a fast race, with more challenges and perhaps the much lauded fatality.

One of the judges' boats zoomed in and butted up against the starting barge. A woman jumped across to the barge and engaged Charlie in a whispered conversation She pointed and waved her arms, and Charlie responded with a *What do you want me to do?* gesture.

"Something is wrong," Ascott said to Shoal. "Hey, Charlie," he said, approaching the official. "What's the problem?"

"It's nothing, just some idiot has driven a boat into the middle of the channel."

"Isn't that dangerous?" Ascott still had Charlie's binoculars, so he raised them and peered out over the moonlit water.

"Dangerous and stupid. They'll get themselves killed."

"It's a big boat, too," the judge said from her boat. "One of them cruisers, owned by one of them city fellas."

Charlie and the judge shook their heads at the idiocy of city folk.

"A big cruiser with blue and white markings?" Ascott said, a sense of dread rising in his throat.

"That's the one. Why, he a friend of yours?" the judge asked.

"No, not a friend. Not a friend at all." Ascott handed the binoculars over to Charlie. "I have to go," he said.

"We doing this thing or what?" Shoal asked when he returned.

"Kalim Aarl's boat is out there in the channel. He's been caught up in the migration. This is my chance to get on board and get Tacus back."

"Are you crazy? You can't go out there, it's the migration. If you drive a boat into that you'll get killed, or worse." Shoal looked furious at him for even suggesting the idea.

"If we don't go now, we'll lose them. They'll either head out to sea, or disappear into the islands."

"Let the Seaguard take care of it," Shoal said.

"There's no time. Like you said, they have their hands full with people celebrating the migration."

"Competitors! Take your starting positions!"

"Go, win the race. I'll work something out," Ascott gave Shoal an encouraging smile.

Nine people lined up: two women and seven men, all with the same grim, focused expression.

A minute passed, then the shell horn blew and all nine plunged into the water.

Charlie began his commentary. "All racers are in the water and making good time for the first of the whales. The field is neck and neck!"

Ascott felt a ball of tension building in his stomach. The idea of Kalim Aari taking Tacus away burned like acid. Forget the treasure, forget everything else, Tacus was his friend and the only company he had day in, day out on the island. He may have failed Charlotte, but he would not fail the lisping parrot.

"No," he said aloud.

A discarded pair of whale running shoes lay on the barge. Ascott strapped them on and tossed his t-shirt aside. Taking a deep breath he ran to the edge of the barge and dived.

Charlie broke off mid-spiel. "What the haberdasher was that?!"

"Man overboard!" someone shouted.

CHAPTER 12

Ascott surfaced and swam hard in the wake of the racers, who were already climbing over the first of the whales. The currents in the channel were strong and the swirling water was colder than he was used to. He pushed on, kicking hard, feeling the milknut-fibre soles of his shoes working like fins against the water.

The surfacing whales blocked his view. Kalim's cruiser was out there somewhere—he just had to find it.

In front of him a massive shape broke the surface, a seemingly endless rolling curve of glistening dark skin, a serpent large enough to swallow the world whole. With a whooshing roar the whale breathed out. Water sprayed down in hard drops around Ascott, who forgot to breathe in his astonishment.

So this is how I die, he thought calmly. Other whales were now surfacing; the outer fringe of the pod blocked his way forward and Ascott plunged into the foam. Approaching a whale that was still on the surface he reached out and gripped the dorsal ridge, pulling himself up in a surge of adrenalin. The cool touch of the night air swept the water from his skin. The milknut fibre sandals gave some grip on the slick surface of the whale's skin. With seconds remaining before the beast dived again, Ascott peered out into the darkness and saw a flickering light out in the channel: Kalim's cruiser, trapped fast by the migrating behemoths.

The whale shuddered underneath him. Ascott crouched and then threw himself forward. He landed with a wet slap against the side of the next whale and clung desperately to the triangular humps that ran down its back. His feet scraped against the leathery hide that flexed and rippled underneath him. With a grunt of effort he pulled himself up and crouched on the beast's back. The light was further away; the whales were taking him in the opposite direction. Leaping again, Ascott slapped down on the broad back of a whale and felt the air punch out of his lungs. Groaning and gasping, he crawled to his feet and leaped again. This time he missed, his fingers scrabbling at the whale's flank as he plunged into a swirling tempest of foam and bubbles.

The whales plunged and surfaced around him. At any moment a house-weight of whale could crash down and crush his skull. The night sky vanished under the shadow of their passing and Ascott swam for the nearest creature. Grabbing hold, he pulled himself out of the water and clung to its lower back, gasping for breath.

In his panic he had gone the wrong way and now had to jump again, this time landing on a younger whale. Without pausing he took three running steps and leaped across the churning chasm to the next beast. This one was much older, its hide roughened with barnacles and the scars of a lifetime spent surviving in the deep oceans of the world. Ascott panted for air as he pulled himself up and ran along the whale's broad back. He felt it begin to dive as he jumped again. Plunging into the water, he draped his arms over the tail of a svelte female, her flukes rising as she dived. A helpless Ascott was thrown skywards and with all four limbs flailing, he dropped down on the whale's far side.

The splash of his landing barely registered in the turbulence. He struggled to the surface, taking a salty breath and then staring in shock as the biggest eye he had ever seen blinked slowly at him. A giant whale, the lead bull of this pod, regarded the tiny human with an incalculable expression. Ascott stared deep into the darkness of the titan's eye and felt a crushing sense of scale. What was he compared to a leviathan like this? The eye contact lasted only a second, but Ascott felt it burn deep inside his mind, the moment inscribing itself on his memory forever.

The whale surged past Ascott, who frantically swam to keep

his head above water. Swimming in the whale's wake he felt the air crack as the giant's tail struck the water with explosive force. The wave and spray sent Ascott tumbling into the side of another whale. He climbed up on to its back and tried to work out where he was.

Two more whales, then there was a break which he could swim through to get to the boat. Maybe. With his arms and legs burning from the effort, Ascott stood up and took a running jump. This time he landed well enough to belly flop spread-eagled on the whale's back. It promptly dived and he scrambled off the other side, jumping into the water and swimming for the next one.

How did Shoal manage to do this twice? In one day? Ascott inhaled salt water and coughed, wishing more than anything that he could have a break, crawl on to something that wasn't moving and just breathe. The next whale curved downwards, sending its tail skyward in the classic slap position. Ascott took a deep breath and dived. Staying on the surface would get him slapped into a bloody paste. Straining against the current he swam down into the dark. Grabbing a bulbous piece of coral for support, he felt the water around him rock with the force of a tail strike. The fish had all gone. *Because they're not stupid,* Ascott told himself.

The song of the whales vibrated through the water around him. They spoke in long melodies, from almost dirge-like moans to shrill whistles, their voices going up and down the scale.

In the swirling aftermath of the tail, loose debris and sand swirled up from the bottom. Ascott lost his air when a limp form spun out of the mist of silt and struck him with a flopping arm. He had time to register the body as one of the male finalists before he needed to push for the surface.

Please let Shoal be all right. If ever there was a time for Drakeforth to make an appearance and do something godly, this is it, Ascott prayed as he broke the surface.

The cruiser was closer now; the whales were swimming past it, or underneath it. The boat rose and fell on the heaving swell as Ascott struck out across the churning water. The running lights and some internal lights shining through the portholes suggested someone was on board. Trying to keep his panting to a minimum, Ascott let the current pull him towards the dive platform at the back of the boat. If Kalim had set a guard, then Ascott was in trouble.

A careful peep over the top of the dive ladder revealed that Kalim didn't think anyone would be able to make it out to the middle of the channel that evening. The deck was deserted.

Climbing on board, Ascott crouched down. The low calls and whistles of the whales singing to each other vibrated through him; and over that noise, he thought he heard the muffled sound of Tacus cursing angrily.

CHAPTER 13

Ascott crouched on the deserted deck, catching his breath and hearing snatches of laughter and voices from below decks. Kalim's dive crew were talking down there and the sound of cutlery on plates suggested they were eating.

Great, Ascott thought. *Now what?* With nowhere else to go, he tried a recessed door at the back of the cabin. The handle twisted and he felt the door slip open under his damp palm. The door opened silently and closed with a slight click after he passed through. The room beyond was decorated in wood panelling and held a curving bench seat with matching table clad in leather upholstery, all coloured in a dark wine-red shade. A glowing chandelier rocked overhead in time to the rise and fall of the boat, sending the shadows swooping like the silhouettes of children playing on a swing.

At the end of the room was a door of flimsy wood and slats, almost like the door to a wardrobe. Ascott pulled it open and peeped through to a narrow corridor. The voices were louder now and laughter punctuated the sounds of dishes. A light came on as a door opened. Ascott pulled back, closing the slatted door to a crack.

"I'll buy you a whole bar!" a sailor said to someone in the room he was stepping out of, to the loud amusement of the others. Ascott waited with his heart in his mouth as the guy turned and stumbled down the corridor away from him on some unknown errand.

Ascott plunged through the door and moved down the corridor.

Somewhere, a toilet flushed. Ascott looked around and tried a door opposite the dining room. It turned out to be a kitchen, which, Ascott supposed, made sense and convenience. *If convenience could be made, rather than just occurring naturally.*

Ascott, he told himself, *you're babbling.*

"I do that when I'm terrified," he muttered.

The door up the hall opened again and Ascott ducked into the kitchen and watched. The sailor came down the narrow hallway and went back into the dining room.

"Hey, where's the javas?" a voice demanded. The sailor stopped and waved a hand.

"Keep your cufflinks on," he said and turned back to the kitchen.

The door opened before Ascott could come up with a genius plan. Instead he squeezed into the space behind the door. When the sailor came into the kitchen, Ascott slipped out behind him and went exploring deeper in the boat.

The first few doors he found were locked. The toilet door smelled like it should stay locked, perhaps permanently. The final door, located at the end of the corridor, opened when Ascott tried it.

This is what people mean when they refer to staterooms on boats, *he thought.*

The room was as large as the deck area at the back, the windows hung with rich fabric drapes; an even grander crystal chandelier swayed from the ceiling and wood-panelled cabinets, some with glass doors, displayed bottles of expensive liquor and crystal goblets. The walls were decorated in homage to pirate fashion, with crossed swords on the walls and a pirate flag showing a white silhouette of a sinking ship over two crossed cannons on a black background: the infamous *Jolly Steve.*

A table to one side was covered in chewed pieces of crayon, scattered sheets of paper and guano. Feathers of various colours were scattered on the floor and from somewhere nearby a familiar voice was singing:

"No matter where—HIC!—we looked

"We couldn'a found her.

"Thacked up with the cook

"That—HIC!—bleedin' bounder

"Now Cap'nsh lyin' on hith bed,

"Flat ath a flounder…"

One of the wood-panelled cabinets shook with a thud from inside. Ascott crouched down and opened the door. Tacus regarded him with one bleary eye from where he crouched in a spreading pool of rum.

"Fin' your own lav—HIC!—lav-tree. Thith oneth occu—HIC!—pied," the parrot scolded.

"Tacus…" Ascott whispered, in concerned relief. "What did they to do you, buddy?" He lifted the drunken parrot out of the cabinet gently and stroked what remained of his once dense plumage.

"They flogged me featherth, Cap'n. Ne'er thaid…Ne'ever thaid nuffin. Thecret'th thafe with—HIC!—me."

"Let's get you out of here." Ascott held Tacus against his chest and then had to clamp his beak shut as the bird launched into another verse of *The Captain's Wife*.

Hearing voices approaching up the hall, Ascott squeezed himself into a storage cupboard. Tacus' head flopped on his shoulder. "I love—HIC!—you man…"

"Shh…" Ascott hissed. The door to the stateroom opened. Ascott heard Kalim's voice. "What a mess. Where did you put the parrot?"

Another voice replied, "In the liquor cabinet. He was trashing the place."

Footsteps strode over the floor and Ascott heard the cabinet door jerk open.

"He's gone," Kalim said. "Find that bird!"

Even in a room as luxurious as the stateroom on Kalim's cruiser, it would take about twenty seconds for someone to wrench open the cupboard door and find them. Ascott mentally prayed for a miracle. *Drakeforth? Arthur? Help?*

There was no immediate response. Tacus roused himself and squawked loudly, "Keep the noithe—HIC!—down out there!"

The door opened and one of Kalim's crew blinked down at them both.

"Surprise!" Ascott shouted and burst out into the room. He struck the sailor with his shoulder and the man went down with a loud *OOPH!*

Kalim yelled and lunged at Ascott, who, with no other ideas, tossed the half-plucked Tacus down the narrow corridor like a long pass in football.

"*Banz—HIC!—haaaiiiiii!*" Tacus shrieked and flapped his wings. His lack of feathers put him into a lateral spin; he torpedoed into the deck, where he flopped onto his back and lay there, giggling.

"So, you think you can steal the treasure map away from me?!" Kalim yanked a sword down from a display on the wall and thrust it at Ascott, who yelped and fell backwards, crashing into a liquor cabinet and sending bottles tumbling across the floor. Kalim roared and stabbed downwards. Ascott picked up the nearest bottle by the neck and it clanged against the sword's blade. Scrambling to his feet, Ascott swung at Kalim's head. The pirate blocked with his sword and took a vicious swipe at Ascott's legs.

Ascott jumped and found himself sitting on the top of the cabinet, swinging wildly with the bottle. An angry slash of the sword and the bottle shattered, spraying white spirits everywhere. Ascott scrambled for a better weapon, his skin stinging from a multitude of nicks and cuts from the broken glass. He grabbed the first thing that came to his hand. A set of metal coasters, stamped with the *Jolly Steve* emblem. They were square and not particularly sharp. Their corners, however, were pointy. Ascott hurled the first coaster and it spun through the air to thud into the wood panelling like a well thrown knife.

Inspired, he threw another one. Kalim moved his head and the coaster clattered against the wall. With a snarl he raised his sword to cut Ascott down.

Ascott chucked the third coaster blindly and Kalim howled in pain, dropping the sword to clutch at his face.

Taking his chance, Ascott ran out the door and slammed it shut behind him. Scooping up Tacus, who immediately squawked

"Again!" Ascott ran to the back of the boat and jumped into the whale-tossed surf.

CHAPTER 14

The water was colder than Ascott remembered and twinges of cramp spasmed through his legs. He surfaced, treading water and lifting Tacus high to keep him as dry as possible.

"Man overboard!" Tacus squawked, his wings flapping uselessly as the swell swept over Ascott's head.

"Ascott!" Shoal yelled. He wanted to call back, to shout that he had done it, he had rescued Tacus, but the water gagged him. He spat it out and took a wet breath. Torchlight swept over the water. The last whale pod had passed, and now the channel was clear the cruiser was moving off, picking up speed and heading for open water.

"Ascott!" Shoal yelled again.

"Parrot overboard!" Tacus yelled, lifting one foot at a time out of the water and trying to climb onto Ascott's head.

The torchlight swept over them, then came back and held the pair in its beam.

"There they are!" Shoal shouted. A boat engine hummed and soon hands were reaching down to pluck them from the water.

"Tacus knows," Ascott said through chattering teeth. "Tacus knows where the treasure is buried."

Charlie drove the boat to the shore of the island of Saint Amoeba. A camp had been set up on the beach to receive the competitors at the end of the race. Whole fish roasted over a warm fire, and plenty of java, were being consumed by the spectators enjoying the after-party.

A medic tended Ascott's wounds as he sat wrapped in a towel

and a blanket near the fire. A gash on his forehead was quite deep and they glued it shut with tree resin before applying a bandage. Tacus lay snoozing in his lap, swaddled in a towel of his own.

After the first aid had been applied, Ascott sat alone on the beach as thoughts gingerly tip-toed around his head, avoiding the more painful parts and talking quietly amongst themselves.

Kalim called Tacus the treasure map.

Tacus likes to draw…amoeba?

Islands?

…Treasure maps?

Shoal came around the fire and sat down next to him.

"What do you mean, Tacus knows where the treasure is buried?" she asked.

"The gold the ship's doctor wrote about in the *Bilgepuppy* log. He said it was a pirate ship and the first Captain Aarrgh was a pirate. He buried his treasure somewhere in the archipelago and then his ship went down in a hurricane. The crew got off somehow and either drowned or disappeared. Only the ship's surgeon went down with the ship. He was the one holding the metal case with the log."

"Well, yeah," Shoal said. "But what does that have to do with Tacus?

"Parrots can live for a very long time. His drawings…I think they are a map. A map of where to find buried treasure."

"You said he was drawing amoeba," Shoal reminded him.

Ascott stood up so fast he almost dropped the towel and Tacus on the sand. "That's it! Shoal, you're a genius!"

She stared at him, one eyebrow raised in a dangerous way.

"Tacus isn't drawing amoeba, he's drawing the island of Saint Amoeba." Ascott said.

Shoal looked around to make sure no one was within hearing distance. "You mean that the treasure is here? Buried on the island of Saint Amoeba?"

"Exactly." Ascott beamed and then sat down hard as dizziness overwhelmed him.

"We can't go digging around on Amoeba, this is sacred land. The only time we are allowed here is during Migration. Even then we're not allowed past the beach."

Ascott looked inland, beyond the partygoers huddled around the flickering fires, where there was nothing but dense forest, the calls of night-birds and the gentle shushing of waves on the sand.

"Well...how would anyone know we were here?" he asked with a sideways look.

"I would know," Shoal said firmly. "I would know and that would be enough."

"But there is treasure here. Right here. And Tacus can draw us a map."

"Maybe the treasure should stay here. Untouched. What good comes from digging up the past?"

"It's a *discovery*. It's begging to be found. That's how it works. Things are lost, maps are found, and then discoveries are made."

"Why can't you just be happy with what you have? Why do you always have to go off and claim everything like it is meant to be yours?"

Ascott didn't have a ready answer to that question, and Shoal didn't wait for him to come up with one. She stood up and storm-ed off through the partying crowd.

"Idiot," Tacus muttered, and yawned before tucking his head under his plucked wing.

Ascott sat there, watching the flames and the people dance. They seemed happy. It wasn't just the java—they seemed genuinely happy. They had witnessed the natural order of things come around again with the whales migrating. They had cheered on their favourites in the races and they had food, drink and someone to dance with.

Does knowing too much make you unhappy? Ascott wondered. Was it simply because he knew an entire world existed beyond the horizons of the islands that he had this urge to catalogue and quantify everything? Did knowing that Charlotte was going to die mean he could have done something to save her? Drakeforth had said it would happen anyway. But what did he know? He was a god who hated religion. He certainly wasn't happy, and if he was a god, he must know pretty much all there was to know.

Ascott gingerly touched his face. The scratches where the

broken bottle had cut him stung, and the glued-up cut under the dressing throbbed. Shoal had been happy before he came along. She knew little of the world beyond the archipelago and was content with her world. Then along came city boy Ascott Pudding, who started imposing order on everything. Making the world change to his view of how it should be. Every fish labelled, named, and described. Every treasure unearthed and the one girl other than Charlotte that he could ever imagine being friends with driven away because it was more important to him that he find a stupid buried treasure than ask her—

Oh…bite my biscuits, *Ascott thought with an inward groan.* You really are a complete idiot.

Ascott stood up, then gently crouched down and put Tacus in his towel nest in a woven basket of leaves.

"Wait here," he said. Tacus snored and clicked his beak.

Hurrying across the san with his blanket flying out behind him like a cape, Ascott smiled and nodded at the dancers who reached out and tried to draw him into the festivities. With the fire at his back and the moon high in the sky he could see quite well. Apart from the occasional staggering party-goer giving a spirited inaugural address to the sand-dunes, the beach was empty.

Ascott ran, ignoring the pounding in his skull. He didn't shout her name, afraid that might drive her away. Instead he headed to the far end of the beach, where the cliffs came down to the sea and extended long snouts of smooth stone into the waves, like giant beasts bending to drink.

Shoal was sitting on a wave-polished boulder, caught in the moonlight in a way that made her hair and skin glow. Her knees were drawn up and her chin rested on her folded arms.

"Shoal," Ascott said, rather recklessly from well within rock-throwing range. "I'm sorry. I've been a complete fool and I apologise. You achieved something wonderful today and I nearly ruined it by doing something stupid. Then, just to make sure, the first thing I do when you rescue me, *again,* is completely ruin it by suggesting something else even more stupid. I'm sorry. I should be congratulating you. You ran the Migration Race twice today, and then you won and I haven't even said congratulations."

"I didn't win," Shoal said, as quietly as the waves stalking the beach.

"What? Of course you won. Isn't that why we're having this party?" Ascott climbed up the rocks and sat next to her. There was plenty of room on top of the round rock, so he chose to sit close.

"No," Shoal said and sighed. "Migration is about more than winning a race. It's about celebrating the return of the whales. The whales come here to give birth and as long as they come, we know that the oceans beyond the horizon are still kind to them. In the old days people marked the passing of the years by the arrival of the whales. We rejoice because as long as they live, there is hope for all of us."

"I didn't know," Ascott said.

"Of course you didn't. You are so focused on looking at the fish you can't see the life that is all around you."

"I need to leave. To go home to the city. I can catch the next flight out. My sister, Charlotte, she's the only family I have, and… she's in trouble. Drakeforth says there is nothing to be done to save her, but that's no reason not to try," Ascott said, staring out at the incoming swell.

Shoal said nothing for a long minute. Ascott wondered if she had heard him at all. Then she lifted her head. Watching the water, she said, "Nana Smith used to tell me the story of the House Crab." Shoal's accent changed and she spoke in the patois of her ancestors. "She would say, "He's a big fella, about the size of your fist. With claws that can cut a man's finger clean off. House crab, he don't like the shell of his own that he growed. So he goes around picking up empty shells and putting them on his back, carrying them around, and when something big enough to eat him comes along he hunkers down and hides under that borrowed shell. Only his big ol' claws sticking out. But then he sees a new shell that he thinks is even better than the one he's already carryin'. So he goes over and picks up this new shell and puts it on top o' his other borrowed shell. Some house crab get so they have three of four shells piled up on themselves. Get to carryin' so much junk they can hardly move.

""People are like ol' man House crab," Nana would say. "They got everything they need right there on their shoulders. But they go around picking up new problems and worries. Putting them on their backs and carrying them everywhere they go. Only difference is people think that goin' somewhere else means they can leave their problems behind. They always act so surprised when they find they carried them with them, jus' like ol' House crab." That's what Nana Smith always used to say."

Ascott considered her words for a while. "Why do you think the House Crab gathers those extra shells? Maybe the females are attracted to larger specimens and the extra shells create an illusion of—" he broke off, aware that Shoal was regarding him with a determined expression.

"It's not a story about crabs dating, Ascott, it's about people. You're supposed to learn a lesson about life from it, not try to analyse it for your book."

Ascott took a deep breath, aware that his legs was going numb on the cold rock. "You're saying that if I leave here, I'll just take my problems with me, like a House Crab loaded up with extra shells?"

"Bongo," Shoal said.

"Did your Nana have any tips on how to get rid of the extra shells folks might be carrying?"

Shoal shrugged. "She didn't have a story for that."

Ascott wrapped his blanket around them both. Shoal's body pressing against his was warm and soft. She laid her head on his shoulder and he could smell all the warmth of the lagoon at midday in her hair. It was the scent of peace and perfection.

"I really thought you were going to win," he murmured.

"So did I. I came second! I missed the last jump and ended up in the water. Lost ten points."

"No way? Can you appeal? Ask for a recount?"

"It doesn't matter. I didn't need to beat everyone else. I needed to know that I had run the race. I did that. I did that *twice*." Shoal pulled the blanket away from Ascott and tighter around herself.

"You sure did," he said.

She didn't reply. Instead she lay down on the wide rock, wrapped in the blanket, and fell asleep. Eventually Ascott lay back on the stone and Shoal murmured in protest and sleepily punched him in the rib.

Ascott stared up at the stars and wondered what to do next.

CHAPTER 15

Drakeforth nudged Ascott with a sneaker-clad foot. Ascott mumbled something and threw an arm over his eyes to block out the morning sun. Drakeforth gave a long-suffering sigh.

"You're awake, Ascott. You're awake and, to prevent undue fuss, you are also fully dressed."

Ascott blinked. He was standing up. A sense of vertigo rocked him and he almost tumbled off the rock. The blanket lay neatly folded by his feet and he was wearing trousers, a shirt and a snap-brim straw hat. Waking up and finding himself in such a state was unsettling.

"These...these are not my clothes," he managed.

"The man makes the clothes," Drakeforth replied. "More importantly, you're an idiot."

"Yes, Tacus said exactly the same thing to me last night."

"An eminently wise old bird. You sat here last night and told that girl you are planning on turning around and running away. Exactly what is that going to achieve?"

"I need to save Charlotte," Ascott said.

"Well, you can't. So stop thinking that you can waste time trying. Instead, try looking at what you have right in front of you."

Ascott looked. "The ocean?" he offered.

"Close enough for our purpose, I suppose. Yes, an entire ocean of possibilities. You need to stop letting opportunities slip through your fingers. Especially when those opportunities don't want to slip through your fingers."

"What does that mean?" Ascott asked.

Shoal surfaced out in the breakers, her head tilted back as she swept wet hair from her face.

"Oh," Ascott said. "Right."

Drakeforth stepped in front of him, blocking the view. "Pay attention. This isn't about her. At least, not like that. Your destinies are linked, but not intertwined."

Ascott nodded and walked down to the water's edge. He handed Shoal the blanket as she came out wearing only her usual kibini top and cut-off shorts. She wrapped herself up and frowned.

"When did you go shopping?"

"I woke up wearing them," Ascott said truthfully.

"Suits you. The hat is a nice touch."

"Thanks."

"Did you mean what you said last night?" Shoal flipped the edge of the blanket up so it covered her head in a hood.

"Which part?"

"About leaving. Going back to the city." Shoal rubbed her wet hair vigorously.

"I...Charlotte is my only surviving family," he said.

Shoal stopped moving under the blanket. "Do you have anything to stay for?" He couldn't see her face.

"Yes. Yes I think I do. I...I have everything to stay for. My research, the encyclopaedia, Tacus, and, uhm...you."

The blanket slid back and Shoal glared at him through her tousled blonde fringe. "What about me?"

"Well I mean...I uhm...the thing is..." Ascott felt his face growing hot under her stare. "I like you? I mean, you're a good friend."

Shoal combed her hair back with one hand. Her blue eyes sparkled. "Mum thinks I should marry you."

Ascott opened his mouth and closed it again.

"Your face!" Shoal laughed. "It doesn't matter what Mum thinks. I don't want to marry anyone right now."

A sharp whistle cut through the conversation. Ascott looked up the beach. Between the remains of last night's fire and a boat bobbing in the surf, a figure was waving.

"We'd better go. Once the last boat leaves, it's a long swim home," Shoal said and walked off along the beach.

The trip back to Montaban was conducted in silence. Tacus raised his head once, gazing with a bleary eye at the pitching horizon, and moaned before burrowing back into his towel nest.

Ascott picked him up, still swaddled, when they stepped off the dock.

"You can bring Tacus to my place if you want. Mum'll have some soup that should help him recover."

"What kind of parrot drinks rum?" Ascott said, regarding the wrapped bundle with concern.

"I don't think he'll be trying it again for a while. I just hope his feathers grow back," Shoal replied.

They walked up the hill. The port was quiet the day after Migration. Everyone seemed to be resting in the shade, nursing their dancing feet and sore heads.

"They will grow back," Ascott said. "Birds moult, new feathers might take a while to grow in, but he'll be back to his old self in...time."

"I never thought I'd say that I miss him constantly barking," Shoal said.

They went into the cool dark of Smith's Dive Emporium. The shop was empty so they climbed the stairs to the house above.

"Mum makes soup the day before, she doesn't like cooking the day after Migration." Shoal turned the stove on and set a large pot on the element.

"I've got loads of Tacus' maps back at my place. I stuck them on the fridge and the walls. But you know, I never paid much attention. Now that I think about it, they all look the same."

"In the log book, that ship's doctor, Dentine Tubule, wrote that they found a great treasure somewhere in the islands. So... if Tacus was there, he could be still drawing maps of where they buried it. On Saint Amoeba."

"I guess so." Ascott stroked the bird's head, making Tacus purr. "Do you have any maps or charts of the islands? I'd like to see what Amoeba looks like."

"Never needed a map before. Most of us keep it up here," Shoal stuck her head through the beaded curtain that hung from the kitchen door and waved a spoon at her ear.

"Someone must have a map of the islands somewhere," Ascott said.

"Maybe the Exco?" Shoal replied from the kitchen.

"I'll check it out later." Ascott sat down. His head still throbbed, and the strange clothes he was wearing felt stifling in the rising heat of the day.

Shoal emerged with bowls of soup; one each for herself and Ascott and a third for Tacus. Ascott roused the parrot and held a spoon of broth to his beak, letting the bird dabble in it with his stone-coloured tongue.

"Curthed liquor," Tacus muttered, and gargled some more soup.

"You shouldn't drink, Tacus," Shoal said, sitting on the sagging couch next to Ascott and curling her legs up under herself.

"I drink to forget," Tacus said mournfully, nibbling the edge of the spoon with his beak.

"What does a parrot need to forget?" Ascott said.

"I can't remember," Tacus said and then threw his head back and gave a squawk of laughter. "They took my featherth," he said. Sobering under the influence of the soup, he preened the thinned remnants along his wings.

"You're safe now, and they will grow back. Think of it as an early moult," Ascott suggested.

"Pluckerth. If I thee them again, I'm going to pluck them up good."

"I think the plucked looks suits you," Shoal said. "Makes you look like a bird not to be messed with."

Tacus preened his few remaining chest feathers and made a happy noise.

They finished their soup in silence.

"Can you look after Tacus while I go down to the Exco?" Ascott said.

"Tacus can look after himself," Shoal said, letting the spoon clatter in her empty bowl.

"Or Tacus can stay here and look after himself and you can come with me to the Exco."

"You'll get further with me than on your own," she said.

The streets were starting to fill with people again, most of them wincing at the daylight and moving quietly. Conversations were whispered, and even the gulls looked sceptical of their chances of a feed from the fishing fleet today.

The Export Company office was open. Shoal said she had never known it to be closed, except at night, and even then you could usually find someone working somewhere in the building.

"They don't lock it up at night?" Ascott asked.

"Why would they? If you start locking things up people start to wonder why you need to, and then they start breaking in to satisfy their curiosity."

"What about the pearls and other valuables?"

Shoal shrugged. "People around here don't steal. If someone needs something, they ask. We share things and look out for each other."

"It wouldn't take much to ruin the perfection of this place, you know," Ascott said.

"Why would anyone want to do that? If we can't convert them to our easy-going ways, we can always take them out into the channel, tie a rock to their feet and drop them over the side."

"Your isolation is your best defence. No one knows how perfect this place is. Even if they did they would never believe it." Ascott held the door open to the Exco.

"Tourists come—and go. That's why they are tourists." Shoal brushed past him and went inside.

The Exco was empty except for a woman stretched out asleep along one wall, her tanned arms wrapped around a wooden horn that might have been a distant cousin to the saxophone. She muttered in her stupor and stirred, making the instrument sigh a middle C note.

The teller was in place behind his iron bars. Today he wore a green visor to go with his starched collar and bow-tie.

"Morning, Sam," Shoal said.

"Hey girl!" Sam beamed carefully at them. "What can I do for you today?"

"I'm looking for any maps and charts of the islands you might have?" Ascott tried to speak quietly so as not to disturb the sleeping woman.

"Maps and charts, eh?" Sam scratched the white stubble on his dark cheeks. "Don't know nothing about maps and charts."

"Nothing back in the file room?" Shoal asked.

"Mebbe…" Sam looked unenthused about the idea of going to check.

"Hey," Shoal said brightly, "Why don't Ascott and I go back there and check and you can tend to your other customers?"

Sam and Ascott both looked around the nearly deserted Exco lobby. The sleeping woman lifted one leg and let out a rumbling note a good octave lower than the horn had managed.

"Well, okay then…" Sam seemed unsure. Moving with a glacial slowness he slid off his stool and moved to the swinging half door that separated the staff area from the public space of the room. With a grunt of effort the withered old man pulled the door open.

"It's been a long time since anyone came back here, there were words…ahh…Welcome to the Export Company Montaban office. Enter freely, go safely and please, no flash photography." Sam closed the swinging door and executed a slow U-turn. They waited while he crossed the floor and reached up for a cobweb-covered key ring on a dusty hook.

"I thought you said that no one ever locked anything up around here," Ascott whispered to Shoal.

"They don't," Shoal replied.

"I always wondered what this key was for. Must be for the file room, eh?" Sam grinned again.

The hunt for the locked door ensued at a speed that would have a tortoise drumming its claws with impatience. Sam conducted a tottering perimeter search, pausing occasionally to move chairs and cardboard cartons. Shoal and Ascott stepped up to help move the heavier items and most of the lighter ones as well. They found blank walls behind furniture, the humming freezer, coat racks, and piles of driftwood that Sam explained "were briefly considered as a form of currency after the oyster plague of eighty years ago wiped out pearl production for a time."

"How would that work?" Ascott asked.

"Well, one idea was to cut the wood up into small discs and paint them a silver colour."

"Did they do that?" Shoal asked, moving a wastepaper bin full of carefully rolled pairs of woollen socks.

"Nope, couldn't find any paint."

Ascott came to the filing cabinet. It sat silently with an air of casual watchfulness as if waiting for someone to invite it to share its years of collected wisdom on a range of subjects.

"Help me move this, Shoal." Ascott crouched down and got his arms around the cabinet. Shoal gripped it at the top and they twisted and turned, walking the heavy thing across the floor. The filing cabinet rattled its drawers, dust puffing from ancient seams in consternation.

"There, there," Sam said with a soothing pat on its flank. "Just a little house-keeping. Nothing to worry about. You know, this filing cabinet was old when I started here."

Ascott couldn't imagine anything older than Sam the teller. He looked like a mummified corpse with a starched collar and bowtie.

"And how old are you, Sam?" Shoal asked with a grin that suggested she knew the answer but liked to humour the old man.

"A hunnert and twenny-two. Born on Migration Day." Sam grinned at Shoal.

"Sam's Montaban's oldest resident. You know he won the Migration Race in his day?"

"More'n once. Course back then there were more whales and they were bigger too. Got so a fella could run the channel without ever once getting his feet wet," Sam chuckled, a dry rattling sound like dice in a cup at the bottom of a crevasse.

"Shoal came second in this year's race," Ascott said.

"So I hear. Fine effort," Sam nodded.

"A door," Shoal said, pointing to the wall space behind the filing cabinet.

"Well shovel my shrimp, how long d'ya think that might have been there?" Sam said, scratching his ear.

"Probably as long as the building has been here?" Ascott suggested.

"Nope, this building was built no more'n thirty migrations ago. Weren't no door here then. "Fore that the Exco was like every other place. Space cut into the white-rock."

"It must have been. You can't just build a door in a wall and put a cabinet in front of it without anyone noticing," Ascott said, peering closely at the door. It was covered in dusty cobwebs, with a large and ornate metal lock plate built into its face, but no apparent latch or handle.

"Try the key in it," Shoal suggested. Sam lifted the key ring with both hands. Ascott took it and slid the key into the hole. Twisting it, he felt the interior workings of the lock grate against each other like a fist full of pebbles.

"It's quite stiff," he said through gritted teeth.

"Let me try." Shoal pushed in and seized the oversized key in both hands. She twisted until the tendons stood out on her arms.

"It's a lampet lock," Sam said with pride. "Haven't seen one of them since I was your age. There's a trick to it."

The old man shuffled forward and put a hand lightly on the key. With the gentlest gesture he twisted it all the way around and the internal mechanism clicked as it released.

"Lampet lock," Sam said again.

"Just like a lampet on a rock. You have to sneak up on them and ease them off. If you pull too hard, they grip with everything they have and you'll never move them," Shoal explained.

"Oh? Well, I haven't started the chapter on molluscs yet," Ascott said with something of a hurt tone.

With the key still in the lock, Sam strained to pull the door open. He stepped back, panting, as Shoal and Ascott took over. The heavy steel door creaked as it swung outwards on disused hinges. A smell of stale salt water and the ghost of damp wafted out through the gap. Beyond the door they could make out the dimensions of a small room. Judging from the apparent age and volume of the contents, all four dimensions had been filled to capacity for some time.

"Well…that's curious," Sam admitted.

"What is this place?" Shoal said, not venturing into the gloom.

"Some kind of old store room. Sam, do you have any battery-powered torches?" Ascott asked.

"Some what now?" Sam cocked his hand to his ear.

"I'll see what I can find." Shoal vanished up to the front of the Exco and returned a minute later with two torches. "They were being used as paperweights," she explained.

The yellow light banished the darkness in its typical fashion. The room was larger than the toilet cubicle on a train, but smaller than the kind of steamer trunk that gives railway porters nightmares.

With curious caution they began to make an inventory of the items found inside.

"I can barely read this," Shoal complained as she pored over a stack of sheets of stiff paper.

"Is that fish-skin vellum?" Ascott said with awe. "I've heard of it, but to actually see it…"

"Heh," scoffed Sam. "Used to see a lot of it. Never saw no paper from trees back then. We'd scrape the skin of a fish till it was so thin you could write on it. That's what we did in my day. My old papa had a page press. Big heavy thing, with a screw handle. We'd be up before dawn clampin' it down on the latest batch of sheets. Squeezin' the juice outta them an' trimmin' 'em up just so."

"It's beautiful," Shoal said, holding up a sheet so the desiccated scales caught the light in a spray of colour.

"You could boil pages into soup if you were desperate, too," Sam added.

Ascott took up a sheet and examined under the torchlight. The ink had faded, but he could make out columns of numbers and names.

"This is something Arthurian," he said. Putting the sheet aside he picked up another one and haltingly read the ancient words: "And on tha sevynth daye, Arthur cayme apon the Malon Farmyr and spaked to hym ov tha glorese ov tha Unyverse. Tha Malon Farmyr offeryd his weres to the Lord, sayeng untoo hym, This shell bee three quarks a pounde. Too wych Arthur denouncyd tha Farmyr as a theeph who cometh betwixt tha oweres ov sunryce and sunsette. His pryce per pounde, beyng robbree dun in syt of tha daye."

"Old copies of Arthurian writings?" Shoal asked. "Fruity…"

"Must date back to when the Arthurian missionaries came blunderin' through here," Sam said. "Oh sure, folks pay attention on the right days, and toss a coin to the bearded ones. But they still follow the old gods in their hearts."

"But why would someone hide Arthurian Tellings in a secret store-room?" Shoal asked, effectively walking up to the elephant in the room and slapping it on the rump.

"What else is in here?" Ascott wondered as they carried stacks of fish-vellum papers out into the light. Excavating the paper revealed wooden chests and statues of various shapes, sizes and materials.

"Oh! It's Old Noodle-Nose!" Shoal exclaimed with delight, hefting a squat statue of a humanoid figure with a head that appeared to have been inspired by an octopus from a mad sculptor's nightmare.

"Who?" Ascott said, regarding the strange statue with unease.

"Old Noodle-Nose—he's a sea-god, he spends his time sleeping in his castle at the bottom of the ocean and then once a year he rises and delivers gifts to all the good children."

"Just the sort of thing the Arthurians disapprove of," Sam warned.

"The Arthurians disapprove of giving gifts to children?" Ascott wrinkled his nose.

"No, the idea of worshippin' strange idols. It doesn't fit with their belief system. They used to be a lot more adamant about it," Sam said, running a finger across his neck in a slicing motion.

"So maybe someone hid all these things in here because they were afraid the Arthurian missionaries would burn it all if they found it?" Ascott rummaged some more and lifted a wooden spear with three thin points at the end.

"Ritual fishin' spear," Sam said. "For ensurin' good luck on a fishin' trip."

Further digging revealed statues of the laughing figure that the Smiths had painted on their wall, a miniature fishing net that Sam confirmed served the same ritual purpose as the spear, and a delicately crafted model of an outrigger canoe, small enough to fit in Shoal's hand. Ascott found a large vellum painting that had escaped their earlier excavations.

"Maybe it's a museum," Ascott said, regarding the artefacts stacked up around them. He lifted the delicate vellum sheet and let the torchlight play across it. The yellow light caught a painted image, now faded with age, showing various figures sitting around a table in some kind of cave-like setting bathed in silver moonlight. They appeared to be playing a card game. Arthur was dealing; to his right was the brown-skinned laughing figure, who had an expression of deep focus on the cards in his hand, and next to him was Old Noodle-Nose, apparently an early riser when a card game was scheduled. Next to the octopus-headed god was a woman with a body of transparent silver whose lower half was hidden in water. The final player was a rough-looking bearded man whose mouth snarled with filed teeth and whose hands were crab claws.

In the centre of the table was a large fish made of gold. It took the form of no species that Ascott could recognise, but it was clear that the golden fish was the prize for which the gathered gods were competing.

"Pysces o' Fayte." Ascott read the crudely painted letters at the bottom of the tapestry. "Pisces of Fate?" he repeated.

"Ne'er heard of it," Sam said.

They laid the vellum tapestry aside and opened the wooden boxes that were the only things remaining unexplored. Each crate revealed more carvings and figurines. There were carved wooden bowls with embossed fish designs, a strange puppet made from chunks of coral with string holding the bits together in such a way that they could be moved to simulate walking, and the long-dried remnants of pieces of burned fish and fruit stuck to a tarnished metal plate.

Ascott wiped the sweat from his eyes. The air in the room was close and stuffy. "What if this is a shrine? Some kind of chapel?"

"Someone set this up to worship all the gods?" Sam said from his position on top of a crate of shells that had been polished until they glowed in an iridescent rainbow.

"It's the fruit," Shoal said. "Totally the fruit."

"Someone really wanted to cover their bets," Ascott said.

"Ne'er seen none of it before," Sam reminded them.

"We still haven't found any maps or charts," Shoal said, bringing the conversation back on topic. "Someone's been doing a lot of drawing, but they haven't drawn a map."

Ascott wiped his face. "Well, you know where all the islands are, and Tacus' drawings will tell us where to go once we get there."

Shoal gave Ascott a look. "I don't know where all the islands are. There's too many of them for anyone to know each one. Besides, Nana Smith used to say that the islands move."

"The islands move?" Ascott felt his credulity creaking under the strain.

"Yeah. They move. At night. When no one's looking." Shoal's tone warned Ascott to not question her Nana's wisdom further.

"That would make sense," Ascott said carefully.

"What do we do with all this stuff?" Shoal gestured to the piles of fish-skin and crates of religious artefacts.

"Ne'er mind it. I'll have a fossick," Sam said and ushered the pair to the door.

"If you find anything about the treasure of Captain Aarrgh, put it aside," Ascott said.

"No worries, lad." Sam firmly pushed them out into the Exco lobby and let the half-door swing shut.

Shoal and Ascott hurried out into the sun, leaving Sam to start returning the papers and carvings to their strange storage space.

CHAPTER 16

After collecting Tacus, who was still nursing his hangover, they boarded Shoal's boat and headed out of the port to collect the various drawings that were stuck to Ascott's fridge.

Entering the island lagoon, Ascott scrambled to his feet in the narrow boat. "Ohh no! No! No!" he wailed as the remnants of smoke drifted across the water from the burned remains of his house.

It wasn't until they landed on the beach that they could truly accept what their eyes were telling them. The three-room bamboo hut that had stood, in Shoal's words, "for quite a while," now floated across the lagoon in black flakes and dying embers. A dark patch on the sand showed where it had stood, and the milknut trees that grew at one end were scorched and grotesquely stunted. Only the metal appliances and water desalination tank remained intact, though all were stained with soot.

"Who…" Shoal said, tears streaming down her face.

"Kalim Aari and his crew," Ascott whispered. Everything he owned had been in that building. "My research. My notes. The encyclopaedia," he said weakly, the thud of realisation hammering down on his skull.

"Pluckerth," Tacus squawked from his spot on Ascott's lap.

They got off the skiff and walked up the beach. The ashes of the hut were still smouldering. Ascott kicked sand over a few small fires. Treading carefully, he tossed aside piles of ash and bamboo embers. "The box is gone," he said.

"They found the old book?" Shoal looked dismayed.

"Aaarrgh!" Ascott screamed at the sky with clenched fists.

Shoal waited till he had gotten it out of his system. "You can stay with us. Mum and Dad will be fine with that."

"Thanks. We need to find that treasure. There's no telling what they might do if they think we have information that we are not giving them."

"So we find the treasure, and then what? The pirates steal it away?" Shoal asked.

"No, we find it and keep it a secret until they give up searching. Then they leave and never come back."

"We *hope* they leave and never come back," Shoal said.

"They will leave. I'll make sure they leave," Ascott kicked another foot's worth of sand over the smouldering pile of his house and turned his back on it all, walking back to the boat.

The return journey to Montaban was taken in silence. Ascott sat in the bow, brooding, while Tacus wrapped his near-naked wings around himself and scowled at everybody. Shoal didn't know what to say. The idea of someone deliberately burning down your house was beyond her comprehension.

Ascott refused her suggestion to report the arson to the Seaguard. Instead they went to the Smiths' house, where Palm made tea and insisted everyone have a second helping of her Migration Day soup.

"Of course you can stay here," Sandy said. "He can sleep on the couch, right?" he looked at Palm, doubt rising on his face.

"Yeah, we always have room for family," Palm almost cackled. Ascott felt a sense of relief that Palm didn't appear to have any plans for taking over the world. He felt sure Shoal's mum would be a formidable evil genius.

They spent the afternoon encouraging Tacus to draw. He didn't cooperate, choosing instead to explore his surroundings and complain about the cold.

"Come on, Tacus, if you draw your picture, you can have a nap wrapped up in a blanket," Ascott pleaded.

"Thoo cold…" Tacus moaned in a ghostly voice from the top of a curtain rail.

Ascott gave up and left a selection of drawing paper, crayons and crackers on the table before going out on the stone balcony and staring moodily out towards the sea.

Shoal came up beside him and swung her legs over the low wall, letting her feet dangle towards the street below. "You're going to go back to Amoeba, aren't you?" she said quietly.

"I don't have any choice. I need to find the treasure and put an end to this."

"Well, if you're going to upset all the gods in the islands and then spend eternity grinding salt at the bottom of the sea, I'm going with you."

"Thanks, but what do we tell your parents?" Ascott looked over his shoulder but Sandy and Palm were both downstairs in the dive shop.

"I could tell them that we're going away for a romantic night of passion beneath the stars." Shoal grinned at the suddenly blushing Ascott. "Or fishing."

"Fishing...yeah." Ascott nodded.

Palm insisted on packing them a picnic and extra blankets. Ascott could feel the heat radiating off his face every time she winked and grinned broadly at him, occasionally chuckling "Fishing, eh?"

They packed Tacus in a towel. He had stopped moaning and eaten a cracker but refused to do more than thoughtfully chew on the crayons they offered him.

Down at the port, things were livening up again. Boats were heading out for an evening's fish and the market stall holders were doing voice exercises in anticipation of the resumption of business tomorrow.

Ascott sat on the picnic basket, facing Shoal, with Tacus between his feet. The parrot still showed no interest in drawing anything. "You draw every day," Ascott said. "The same thing, over and over again. Why have you stopped?"

"Pluckerth," Tacus squawked.

"Maybe he's too upset to draw," Shoal said.

"What's he got to be upset about? It wasn't his house that got burned down!"

"Yeah it was. And he lost most of his feathers."

"Pluckerth!" Tacus squawked again.

Ascott lapsed into silence as they turned south, following the winding channel through the islands. Around them the last of the whale pods swam through the channel, surfacing and blowing water into the air as they passed. Ascott watched them and embraced an unaccustomed sense of peace. Here was the natural order of things; the whales following the trails of their ancestors, coming to these islands every year without having to queue to board a flight, or deal with lost luggage. The whales had no anxiety about lost passports or forgetting to lock the front door.

They moved on through the shifting light of the late afternoon, the small boat and the whales, each going their own way, each with an end goal in mind.

Shoal cut the engine ten metres out from the shore of the Island of Saint Amoeba. She frowned at the dense jungle and white sand beach. "We really shouldn't be doing this," she warned.

"I don't have any choice. You can wait here if you want." Ascott stood up and the boat rocked under his shifting weight.

"I'm not letting you go there on your own. There's man-eating turtles and mozzies that'll suck you dry, meat-eating plants and ghosts."

"Ghosts?" Ascott tried to keep a straight face.

"Yes, ghosts. Mostly of people who went on the island when they shouldn't and ended up being eaten by the turtles, or drained of all their blood by the giant mozzies, or grabbed by the plants."

"What about the ones that got scared to death by the ghosts?" Ascott asked.

Shoal scowled at him. "Them, too," she said. "We should get ashore before nightfall."

"Is that when the ghosts come?" Ascott grinned.

"Sure, laugh it up now, city boy, but you'll be sorry when a turtle is nipping your bloodless toes while a trapdoor plant melts you and the ghosts come to steal your soul." Shoal paddled the boat towards the narrow strip of pale sand. Ascott jumped out and ran a line and stake up the beach. Pressing the stick into the ground, he secured the boat against shifting tides.

Ascott and Shoal gathered their supplies. Tacus, wrapped in his towel, settled in a milknut fibre bag that Shoal carried slung over her shoulder.

"What are we looking for?" Shoal asked as they left the beach and climbed the low dunes into the dense jungle.

"I have no idea," Ascott admitted. "I hope we will know it when we find it, though."

As the sun set they climbed over rocks sculpted by wave-driven sand until they were as smooth as giant grey pearls and moved into the undergrowth. It was an alien world, as different from the water as outer space. Ferns rose from the ground, exploding in sprays of green leaves and tightly curled shoots that almost glowed with life. From the larger trees curtains of moss hung in waterfalls of green and yellow. There was no path that they could see, so they pushed their way through the overgrowth, climbing over fallen branches and stumbling through tangled knots of roots and vines that seemed to reach for their legs to drag them down into the soft mulch of the jungle floor.

After half an hour of slogging through the dense foliage their legs were stinging from the scratches of branches. The sweat dripped from them both and they stopped to drink water from the canteen Palm had included in their picnic pack.

"If we were looking for lots and lots of trees, I would say we are on the right track," Shoal said.

"There must be some sign. Can you remember anything that Tacus drew on his maps?" Ascott panted in the humid heat, occasionally slapping at insects that seemed drawn to the scent of warm human.

"He drew some kind of shape with marks going around one side, and there was a blob at the end of the line. I think there were also some other marks—squiggles, mostly."

"When you say it like that, it makes me wonder if the map would be any use to us at all."

"If we knew which side of the map was north, we could look for a trail on the same side of the island as the squiggle," Shoal said.

"Let's assume that the map is on a north—south orientation. So...that way would be north." Ascott pointed into the jungle.

"It's that way," Shoal said, shouldering her bag and walking off in a different direction. Ascott followed her without argument. They wandered through the dark jungle, torchlight standing in for the moon that hid behind the canopy.

"What would the trail look like?" Shoal's voice came from the gloom.

"It would have grown over by now." Ascott looked around from where he had been examining the trees for any scars or blaze marks.

"So flat stones in a row wouldn't be a sign?" Shoal asked.

"What? Where?" Ascott pushed through a tangle of ferns to find Shoal studying the ground.

"Flat stones," Shoal said again. Her torch lit a path of rocks that led off in a winding trail through the brush and trees.

"It cannot be that simple," Ascott said.

"Why not? Not everything in life has to be an insurmountable challenge." Shoal stepped from stone to stone, almost skipping along the narrow path, Ascott on her heels. The path almost vanished several times where the jungle had reached out with green fingers and brushed dirt and leaves over the stones. They followed the line of rock slabs to a wall of green.

"There must be some great nutrients in the soil around here. This stuff is crazy," Ascott panted in the moist heat.

Shoal pulled at the matted branches and leaves. "We could try going around it," she said.

"With the jungle this dense around here, we may never find the path again."

Shoal sighed and wiped her hands on her shorts. "If Tacus still had feathers he could fly over the top and tell us where to go."

"A great idea." Ascott opened Shoal's satchel and lifted the bundled bird out. "Wake up, Tacus," he said, rubbing the parrot gently on top of its head.

"Five more minuteth," Tacus mumbled, his head clamped under one ragged wing.

"Come on, wake up! We need you to show us the way to the treasure," Shoal said.

Tacus' head popped up and he peered at the close and whispering jungle.

"Where are we?" he squawked, his wings stretching and flapping to keep his balance.

"The island of Saint Amoeba. You know, the place you draw all the time."

"Oh no! Get uth out of here! Quick! Run for your liveth!" Tacus flapped his wings desperately but couldn't get any lift.

"It's okay, Tacus, no one else is here. It's just you, me and Shoal. We're perfectly safe." A blood-curdling moan echoed through the foliage. The sound rose in pitch until it became the shrill whistling scream of someone being disembowelled with a dinner plate.

"Catht off! Catht off!" Tacus shrieked. Shoal looked ready to take that advice but Ascott clamped the parrot's beak shut.

"Shhh..." he said.

"Mggh Fhhgghh," Tacus replied.

"You wait here. I'll see if I can find a way through..." Shoal forced her way into the curtain of ferns and tangled branches. In seconds she had disappeared from view.

"Shoal?" Ascott struggled with Tacu,s who was trying to climb on to his head.

"I'm he—!" Shoal's reply broke off into a shrill scream.

"Shoal!?" Ascott let Tacus go and plunged into the dense thicket after her. Tacus crouched on a path stone for a moment, listening to the chilling moan as it rose again, and then he trotted after Ascott.

CHAPTER 17

"Shoal?" Ascott crawled through clinging bushes and snarled knots of creeper and moss. "Shoal?"

"Down here." Her voice sounded oddly distant. "Can you see my torch?" A yellow beam of light played upwards through a buzzing cloud of insects and Ascott pushed his way towards it.

"Are you okay?" he called, lying on his stomach and peering down into a rough hole in the ground.

"I bruised my bum, but other than that I'm fine. You should come down. There's a cave."

"Don't you mean, "You should come up, there's a cave'?" Ascott shone his torch into the hole. Shoal waved up at him, about twelve feet below.

"It's okay. I haven't seen any snakes. Based on their size, I think the spiders probably ate them all," she said.

"Do we have any rope?" Ascott asked.

"Mum packed for a picnic and a romantic night under the stars. Oysters we have, but I think rope was a bit adventurous, even for her."

Tacus hopped up Ascott's back and teetered on his head, "Thoal?" he squawked.

"I'm fine, Tacus, see? Now tell Ascott to come down."

Tacus stretched his wings and leaped. The aerodynamic profile of a bird without feathers bears a striking resemblance to that of a walrus. He screamed all the way down. Shoal caught him and cradled the trembling parrot against her shoulder.

Ascott tucked the torch inside his shirt and slid feet-first over the edge. Gripping a gnarled tree root, he felt his way down the side of the hole.

"We *are* supposed to follow the path," Ascott said.

Shoal shone her light around the narrow cavern. "Why? We don't know where it leads, and this is more interesting."

With Shoal and Tacus leading the way, they headed down the stone passageway. The flag stones here were natural rock formations; water had flowed through the cave and left smooth steps of honey-coloured rock.

From ahead came the low undulating moan rising a terrifying shriek, but this time they heard the surge of the sea underneath the cry.

"Blowhole," Shoal said.

"Pardon?" Ascott blinked.

"The sea pushes air up through holes in the rocks, and sometimes it makes noises. What we are hearing is a blowhole."

At the end of the stone passageway lay a round pool of water lit by the moonlight shining down through a circular hole in the roof. The surface of the pool glowed like silver and cast an eerie white light across the stone walls.

"Bad plathe," Tacus whined.

Shoal stepped forward. Resting one hand on the smooth stone, she touched the surface of the pool. "It's beautiful," she whispered. Her voice echoed around the chamber, amplifying and repeating until a chorus of whispers spoke from every direction.

The water rippled and rose up in a column from the centre of the pool. Shoal and Ascott stepped back, wondering if the ghostly wailing of the wave surge was responsible for the vortex reaching up through the perfect stream of moonlight. "Oh, ship," Tacus muttered, and hid his head under his wing.

The pillar of water refined itself into a human figure. A woman, with water flowing over her features, and her lower half skirted in a flowing tide of silver liquid.

Her watery gaze fell upon them and moist lips parted. "Hello," she said in the voice of water flowing into a teacup.

"He—Hello," Ascott replied. Shoal stood silent, her eyes wide with amazement and a wide grin spreading across her face.

"I have nothing for you. Nothing, for such a very long time," the water woman said, tears falling from her cheeks like the first drops of spring rain.

"We...we came looking for the treasure," Ascott said, unsure how else to explain the intrusion.

"All gone, many, many tides ago. This was once the source of it all. Now, it is a place of memory and sorrow." The water woman stroked the surface of the pool with her glistening fingertips, sending patterns of light swirling through the water.

"Who took the treasure? What was it? Where did they take it?" The questions tumbled from Ascott, his mind a blur with the desperate need to know.

"Men, like you. It was everything, the source. That from which all things flow, the Pisces of Fate. They did not take it far. My power was still something then, and the hurricane that came down upon them destroyed their wooden ship. Where they went from there, I could not follow."

"Are you really her?" Shoal asked.

"I am She," the water woman replied.

"She, The Lady of The Sea," Shoal said to Ascott. "Sailors and fishers make offerings to her before going out."

"Really? She is real?"

"She is She," Shoal said.

"Are you a god?" Ascott asked the wet woman.

"I am the personification of a desire. The thought made real. Why do you look so uncertain? You are more wondrous than I. You who are born of the stars."

"Hardly," Ascott said. "My parents were just normal people, with jobs and a mortgage."

"We followed a treasure map. It led us here," Shoal said.

"The treasure is gone." The flow of water down the woman's cheeks may have been due to tears, or the fluid nature of her form.

"Yes, you said that it was not taken far. Any more clues?"

"The treasure still lies within these waters. It can be found. But be warned, if you seek it, you must be prepared to find it."

"Well, of course we are prepared to find it, that's why we're looking for it," Ascott said in a sharper tone than he intended.

"Thank you!" Shoal called as the lady of the sea began to sink into the silver lit pool.

"This water is still blessed," the lady said. "Your friend may be restored." She vanished, her face spreading and sinking in a final ripple.

"What friend?" Ascott said to the still water.

"I think she means Tacus," Shoal replied. "Legend says the waters where She appears can heal the sick and injured."

"Worth a shot, I suppose," Ascott shrugged, and stroked Tacus on the back of his plucked neck. "Tacus, bath time."

"Than't," Tacus said, his voice muffled under his wing.

"Come on, just a little splash," Ascott knelt down and extended his arm out over the water with Tacus nested in his palm.

"Than't!" Tacus squawked and in a fluttering scramble he ran up Ascott's arm and flapped on his shoulder.

Shoal grabbed the bird and held him firmly in both hands. "Take a breath," she warned.

"Don't wanna," Tacus croaked. Shoal shrugged and stepped to the edge of the water. With the grace of one who spends their time balancing on wave-tossed boats she crouched and plunged the shrieking parrot into the pool. A stream of bubbles erupted from the water. Shoal swished Tacus back and forth for a few seconds and then pulled him out.

"Bath!" the bird howled in anguish. "Baaaath!"

"Oh, you big chicken," Shoal said. Tacus' beak snapped shut and he regarded her with a cold eye.

"Chicken?" he asked. "Chicken?" his voice rose in incredulous anger. "I, madam, am no chicken!" Tacus shook his body like a wet dog, drops of water spraying everywhere.

"Look at his feathers," Ascott said in shock. As Tacus preened himself with what little dignity he could muster, rainbow shades of plumage swelled from his quivering body and in moments stood out in their full previous glory.

Shoal squealed in delight. "Tacus! Your feathers have grown back!"

Tacus flapped and stretched his wings, inspecting each feather in turn. He seemed satisfied that nothing was out of place.

"It's a miracle," Shoal said. "Thank you, Lady of the Sea," she said to the still waters.

"There's a perfectly reasonable scientific explanation for this." Ascott said. Shoal turned and looked at him with one eyebrow arched. "I admit, it's not immediately obvious what that explanation is, but one must exist."

"We should leave here now, before you say something really stupid," Shoal said.

Tacus flapped his wings, feeling the air catch under his restored feathers. He leaped into the air, circled the pool twice and flew out the hole in the roof, silhouetted for a moment against the bright moonlight before vanishing into the circle of dark sky.

CHAPTER 18

After climbing up the roots to the surface they agreed to go back to the beach. The flat stone pathway might go somewhere, but they knew the treasure—what She called the Pisces of Fate—was no longer on the island. The return journey through the clinging jungle took less time now that they knew which way to go.

Shoal felt filled with light. She had been face to face with the Lady of the Sea, one of the old gods. Her faith in the beliefs of her ancestors was confirmed and the joy of that connection with Nana Smith and her line stretching back to the first canoes that came from *Somewhere Else*, that mystical place whose name had been lost to the eroding ravages of time and a focus on oral tradition for recording history rather than something more durable, like stone tablets.

Ascott, on the other hand, kept muttering about optical illusions, swamp gasses and refraction variants of light through mediums with differing densities. In spite of his focus on objective reasoning, one clear thought held centre stage for a solo that deserved a standing ovation: *If the pool can heal and restore anyone, then the sooner I get Charlotte here, the better.*

When they reached the beach, someone had lit a fire on the sand, using Shoal's boat as kindling.

"Oh come on!" Ascott yelled. "What is with this guy and burning other people's boats!?"

A pair of large figures stepped out of the jungle, spear guns aimed at Ascott and Shoal.

"Come on over," Kalim Aari called from the other side of the fire. "We have mushymellows and beer!"

Prodded forward by the spear guns, Shoal and Ascott walked down the beach. Kalim sat in a deck chair, a crumpled straw hat tilted back on his head. His boat was barely visible, moored off the beach, and an inflatable zip craft bobbed in the soft shush of the light breakers.

"Good evening Ascott and...I don't believe I have had the pleasure?" Kalim stood up, extending a hand and a charming smile in Shoal's direction. She wrinkled her nose as though his fingers with dripping with week-old fish intestines.

"This is Shoal," Ascott said. "Kalim, I sincerely hope you have put your affairs in order. That was Shoal's boat you burned this time."

"What, that old wreck?" Kalim laughed. "I figured it was driftwood."

Shoal's eyes flashed in a way that made the fire seem temperate. "It was my Nana's boat," she said through gritted teeth.

"Well, I am truly sorry. Mushymellow?" Kalim handed her a thin stick with one of the toasted savoury treats melting on the end.

Shoal smiled sweetly, took the stick and tossed into the fire, where it flared blue and spat stevia sparks.

"Well, that wasn't called for. That wasn't called for at all." The charm left Kalim's face in a sudden stampede the likes of which had not been seen since the tourists on the cruise liner *Eptatretus* departed the All-You-Can-Eat buffet during a particularly rough passage after Mrs Limpkiss, who suffered from sea-sickness, discovered a soiled sticking plaster in her ambrosia.

Ascott stepped between them. If he lifted his chin he could almost look Kalim directly in the eye.

"What do you want this time?" Ascott asked coldly.

"I want you to tell me what this book means." Kalim turned away and lifted the old journal from a beach-bag next to his chair. "I mean, seriously, I have read this thing from cover to cover. Either pages are missing or someone is making a fool out of me."

"That wouldn't be too hard," Shoal snapped.

"Your words wound me, they really do," Kalim replied. "Now,

I'm not a patient man, so I suggest you tell me what the secret of the journal is, or I will instruct the Citronella twins to shoot one of you somewhere extremely agonising, but not immediately fatal, with a spear gun." Kalim gestured to the two men standing on the edge of the fire light. They raised their spear guns and took aim, one at Shoal, the other at Ascott.

Ascott's throat went as dry as the sand above the high-tide mark. "I'll need to take a look at the book," he said.

"Oh, absolutely, please take your time. Study it, commit passages to memory. In fact, why don't you take it home for the weekend and read it thoroughly!?" Kalim's voice rose to an angry shout and he waved the journal in Ascott's face.

"If you want answers, I need to know what the questions are," Ascott said.

Shoal turned and glared at the two guards over her shoulder. "You boys had best shoot me in the heart. If I'm still alive when I hit the sand, you are really going to regret it."

"You must have worked something out. You came here, didn't you?" Ascott said to Kalim.

"Well, that was easy, see I paid some guy at the docks a few pearls and asked him where you might have gone. Turns out that he heard from a drinking buddy, who heard it from his cousin's wife, who was visiting her sister, who happened to be bringing her laundry in from the balcony line next to the Smith's Dive Emporium and overheard you talking about coming out here. I must admit, it is a beautiful spot. I am sorry about the way I have completely crushed the romantic mood. Really I am."

"I need to see the book," Ascott said again.

Kalim regarded him for a moment, then shrugged and slapped the slim volume into Ascott's open hand.

Ascott turned his back and walked over to the fire. He stood in the firelight turning the pages, and then he lifted his head. Holding the book out in one hand he held it close, but not too close, to the flames.

"Let her go or I burn the book," he said, loud enough to be clear.

"What? What are you doing?" Kalim stood open-mouthed, a

fresh beer bottle glistening with condensation gripped in his hand.

"I said, let Shoal go or I burn the book!"

The Citronella twins turned like two elephants in an elevator, narrowly avoiding tangling the razor-sharp tips of their spear guns as they took fresh aim at Ascott. He feinted dropping the book into the flames. "Let her go! If this book burns, you will never know the secret!"

"Really?" Kalim looked around the empty beach in apparent disbelief. "This is your plan? Wouldn't it be so much easier to just cooperate? You tell me what I need to know, I give you a cold beer, take you home on my boat. I might even arrange for a replacement for the one that I burned!"

"Two. Two boats you've burned, and a house," Shoal said in a voice that could cut glass.

"Right…right…I forgot about that one. That was more of a dugout canoe, how hard can they be to make? You just cut down a tree and chisel out the insides." Kalim shrugged.

"Two boats, one house, *and* you kidnapped Tacus," Shoal added.

"The parrot? The parrot was not kidnapped! That was simply me reclaiming my own property!" Kalim waved his hands in the air, beer spilling into the sand. "He was supposed to have a map tattooed on his body. But no. As useless as a boggle on a wentwhistle."

"Your property? Since when? He's been happily living with Ascott for over a year now. In the house that you burned down! I can't believe you pulled out all his feathers because you thought he was a map!" Shoal looked ready to punch Kalim in the nose. His sudden smile stopped her.

"Forget it, where is the old duck anyway?" Kalim drank the contents of the bottle in his hand.

"He's…he's at home," Shoal said.

Kalim watched her face for a several heartbeats, "Okay," he said. "Okay! Boys, take the girl to the zip-boat, she can take it back to Montaban. See?" he said, turning back to Ascott, who was still holding the fluttering pages over the fire. "I'm letting her go."

Ascott didn't move. His attention seemed captured by the pages of the old log book suspended over the fire. The Citronella twins urged Shoal towards the rubber boat. She got in and started the outboard engine, which hummed with enthusiasm to be off.

The closest twin put his large foot against the boat's rubber side and pushed it out into the water. Shoal sat watching the beach, hand on the throttle but not ready to leave until she saw how things played out.

"There you go," Kalim said, "she's safe and sound and on her way home. Now—the secret of the book, if you please?"

Ascott tensed, digging his toes into the sand and watching Shoal. She nodded and he dropped the book into the flames, where it burned in a flash of heat and light.

"No! No! No! No!" Kalim had a tantrum right there on the beach. He slapped his head, tearing off his straw hat and kicking sand as he howled with rage.

The moment the book left his hand Ascott ran for the boat. Shoal was already gunning the throttle and he dived for the nearest pontoon as the bow lifted under the surge of power. Shoal reached over and pulled Ascott onto the rubber deck, Kalim's screams of fury echoing across the channel behind them.

"I hope Tacus is okay," Ascott said from the floor of the boat.

"Tacus can fly, and if we don't get out of here, we'll wish we could too." Shoal leaned forward, the outboard motor whining as the throttle was squeezed tight. The small boat bounced over the light swells and hit the water with a wet clapping sound.

Ascott sat up. Looking over Shoal's shoulder, he could see the fading glow of the beach fire. There was no immediate sign of pursuit. "I suppose they are in no hurry. They know where you live," he said.

"They'll have to give up now. They don't have the book, and we don't know where the treasure is, either."

"I'm sorry about your Nana's boat," Ascott said.

Shoal grinned and patted the rubber pontoon. "It's okay. I have a new one."

CHAPTER 19

In the middle of the night Montaban was quiet, except for the snores of the inhabitants and the nightly meeting of the Montaban Council of Cats. Felines had been a part of the port town since the first canoes arrived. They had staggered ashore from the boats and found the warm stone, tropical sunshine and abundance of fish-scraps to their liking. The locals were accommodating, for as far as they knew the cats kept the rodent population down and didn't bother anyone. The cats soon established their own hierarchy of rule. At the top were the Alpha Male and the Alpha Female. Below them was a tangled family tree of offspring and other cats that fought for dominance and their place in the ladder of society. The humans, of course, were not considered worthy of inclusion in this government system, ranking with all other living creatures as beneath the contempt of even the lowest cat.

For hundreds of years the Council of Cats watched over the town. Some nights they gathered to debate issues of philosophy and scholarship. Other nights they would simply argue over a point of law or complain about the way kittens didn't show respect for their elders the way *they* did when *they* were that age.

During the day the cats stretched out along the white stone balconies and rooftops of the houses to meditate in the warm sun. In the evenings they dined on fresh fish and the occasional unlucky rat while they watched the town work according to their master plan,* all the while congratulating themselves on being lords of their domain.

---

* The cats of Montaban realised long ago that if a man is given a fish, he feeds you the scraps for a day. If you teach a man to fish, you get

"What was that?" Ascott started at the sound of a banshee choking on a fish bone somewhere around the Montaban docks.

"Just cats," Shoal said. "Help me with this tarp." They pulled the canvas cover over the inflatable boat and left it parked among other, lesser vessels of wood and metal.

"Cats—now there's an animal that knows more than they let on," Ascott said as they climbed up on to the dock.

"Cats know two things: how to steal fish and how to make more cats."

"There's your parallel to humanity right there…" Ascott trailed off.

"What's that supposed to mean?" Shoal was still in a fighting mood after their run-in with Kalim and the Citronella twins.

"Just something someone told me recently. About fish and people and—well, cats too, I guess."

"I'm going home," Shoal said.

"I'm sorry," Ascott said again. "About your boat and everything."

"So am I. But you know, sometimes you have to let old things go and embrace new ones."

"Do you think Nana Smith would understand? About her boat I mean?"

"Nah, she'd hunt that beggar down and use him for shark bait." Shoal grinned. "We had an adventure! We found a living spirit of the old religion and Tacus got his feathers back. Over all it was a fruity date."

"I need to go home—to the City, I mean. I can bring Charlotte back here and we can use the water in that pool to cure her."

Shoal nodded. "I thought you didn't believe in She?"

"Science has nothing to do with what I believe, and everything to do with what I observe," Ascott replied.

"But you believe what you see? Come on, Mum and Dad will want to hear the story from both of us."

free fish for life. This was the basis of the master plan. Many generations later the cats agree all their hard work has been a resounding success and they deserve a nap for their cleverness.

The streets of Montaban were deserted and dark at this hour of the night. Even the pubs which lined the dock as a barrier between sea-business and wife-business were closed. Only the occasional person lay snoring in a stupor, curled in a doorway if they were lucky, face-down in the dirt if they were not.

The cats watched them pass with expressionless faces; only the gleam of their yellow eyes suggested Ascott and Shoal's movements were being observed and included in some grand calculation.[†]

Ascott was going to comment on how the cats around here were distinctly unnerving when an insistent *Pssst!* broke the silence. Shoal nudged Ascott and pointed towards the Exco.

Sam was lurking in the shadows of the barely open door. He gestured for them to come closer before vanishing inside.

The air of the darkened office carried a lingering scent of aniseed. Ascott and Shoal shuffled closer together in the gloom, which reached an even deeper pitch when the door closed behind them. Bright light filled the foyer as if someone had flicked a switch. Sam rubbed his hands together. "Crazy, ain't it?" he said, waving at the flickering chandelier over their heads.

"Sam, did you find something?" Ascott said.

"Sure did. None of it makes a shell bit of sense of course. But that's your problem, I guess."

They followed the old man through the half-door to the office area behind the Exco service counter. Ascott gave him a hand and they pulled the hidden door open. The room looked much like it had when they first saw it, stacked high with boxes of fish-skin parchment and odd artefacts of ancient belief systems.

Sam tottered inside. "I was wonderin' who in the hubris would feel the need to be worshippin' *all* the gods. Seems there's only one fella crazy enough to do that." He rifled through a pile of skins and lifted one up to the light shining in through the open doorway. "Here, take a look at this." Sam handed the crackling sheet over to Ascott.

"I can't make much of it out, the ink has run...Near the bottom

---

† The calculation can be expressed as: $\frac{-b \pm \sqrt{b^2 - 4ac}}{2a}$ because cats and algebra are both inscrutably mysterious.

it says 'Forgive me', and it is signed 'Dentine Tubule'. Dentine Tubule put all this together?" Ascott slowly looked around the room. "But...I found his body in the wreck of the Bilgepuppy."

Shoal scooped up more parchment and scanned them. "Signed 'Dentine Tubule'. For a dead guy he sure found plenty of time to write his memoirs."

"No," Ascott said, "this doesn't make any sense. You can't have the skeleton of a dead ship's surgeon holding a box at the bottom of the sea and at the same time have him gathering artefacts and storing them in a hidden room at the back of the Exco!"

"You think that's freaky? Wait here." Sam shuffled out of the room.

Shoal and Ascott blinked at each other. "What...?" Ascott said to the empty space where the old man had stood a moment before. They listened to the crashing sound of things falling down in the outer office and then the hurried slap of Sam's bare feet bustling across the floor.

Raising a large framed portrait in the doorway, Sam announced from behind it: "Dentine Tubule."

"Dentine Rictus Tubule, founder and first manager of the Montaban Export Company," Ascott read from the faded plaque along the bottom of the frame.

"So Dentine started the Exco, then went off and got himself drowned when Captain Aarrgh's ship sank?" Shoal looked puzzled.

"Nope," Sam said, setting the portrait down with a grunt. "Mister Tubule opened and ran the Exco for years after Cap'n Aarrgh disappeared. Papa always said he was an odd fella. Nervous type. Wouldn't go near the sea. Deathly afeared, he was."

"Weird," Shoal said.

"If he knew about the treasure, why did he stay here? Why not just get rich and go back to the mainland?" Ascott walked around the small storeroom until he reached the cabinet that took up most of the back wall. With the boxes of papers and the village of statues and figures that blocked access now moved out of the way, the cabinet could be opened. He twisted and pulled on the latch. Somewhere deep in the wall, stone ground against stone and then clicked like a giant's knuckle cracking. The entire cabinet swung outward half an inch on hidden hinges.

"I knew it!" Sam cackled. "Executive washroom! They said it didn't exist. But ol' Sam believed!"

A strong smell of seawater wafted through the crack on a draft of cool, damp air.

"Why would you need a secret door *inside* a secret room?" Ascott asked.

"To keep something more secret than secret?" Ascott pulled the door open. "Whoa..." he said.

"Fruity," Shoal whispered with wide eyes.

"Durnit. Toilet's backed up." Sam scowled.

Beyond the secret door in the secret room was a wall of water. It pulsed and undulated gently, like the surface of the ocean turned on its side.

Ascott reached out and carefully touched the shimmering curtain with his finger. The surface rippled and his finger came away wet. "The sea," he said. "The bottom of the sea is behind this door."

"I'm sure there's a scientific explanation for this, too," Shoal said with a grin. Ascott just turned and looked at her, a stunned expression on his face.

"Sam, what is behind this wall?" Ascott asked.

"Glyph Street," Sam replied. "Flinty's pub's on t'other side o' the road."

"Not the bottom of the ocean, then." Ascott went back to peering into the clear water. "I can see fish," he said.

Shoal pressed up against the sea wall, staring through the water-door.

"I wonder where this is," Ascott said.

"Only one way to find out," Shoal replied. She took a deep breath and plunged through the doorway. Swimming in a slow circle, she waved to the startled Ascott before vanishing upwards in the night-dark water.

"We have to help her! What if she can't get back!" Ascott hesitated on the threshold.

"Heh, that girl was born half-fish," Sam scoffed. "She's as likely to drown out there as you are in here."

Ascott stared into the dark water for a while. "Sam, can you get me parchment and a pencil? And if you found a map of the islands, that would help, too."

Sam grunted and shuffled off to see what could be scrounged. Ascott went through the boxes of papers, putting aside fish-skin sheets that caught his eye and dropping the rest in a growing pile on the floor.

After several minutes Shoal reappeared. First her hand pushed through the water-door and then she pulled herself through, dripping wet and laughing.

"It comes out near the *Bilgepuppy*," she said. "The wreck's just on the other side of that reef."

"Tubule can't have been living in a shipwreck at the bottom of the sea and then coming in here on a daily basis." Ascott looked around the room, his sense of the rational crumbling.

"Of course not, he were a man, not a fish," Sam declared, returning with a carved stone mug packed with pencils and a rolled-up sheet of parchment. "B'sides, the fella hated water. Whoever put this door in, it weren't him," Sam said.

"So…is this room in the Exco building, or is it at the bottom of the sea?" Ascott looked up at the ceiling, waiting for it to collapse and flood the entire island.

"It's both," Shoal suggested.

"Pencils and t' chart. I found one of them tourist maps. Wouldn't trust it to keep me off a reef at high tide," Sam said, unburdening himself of the supplies. Ascott took a pencil and began to write a note on a parchment scrap.

"Do you know why I burned the journal?" he asked Shoal as he scribbled.

"Because you were trying to save our lives?"

"Well, yes, but I saw something in it. Something that I didn't want Kalim Aari to know about."

"Numbers?" Shoal asked, looking at the notation Ascott had copied out on the page.

"Map numbers. If we lay a grid on a map, we can find a place by lining up the point in space with the numbers on the map."

"Why not just know where places are?" Shoal asked.

"Because then you wouldn't need a map," Ascott said. Looking up, he added, "Do you know where Captain Aarrgh buried the Pisces of Fate?"

"Well, no, but—"

"I do," Ascott said. Unrolling the map he began to run his fingers over the faded blotches and lines that marked the thousand islands of the Aardvark Archipelago.

"So where's t' bloody treasure?" Sam pushed past them and peered closely at the map.

"Here…I think," Ascott stabbed at the map with a finger.

""Tis nowt there," Sam glowered.

"Here…ish," Ascott corrected.

"No good to no un' there," Sam grumbled.

"We can start looking there. The map…well, it might not be accurate. There are hundreds and thousands of islands in the archipelago. No one could have mapped them all."

"No, but people would know where every rock and one-tree island is. Especially someone old enough to have been sailing these waters for decades…" Shoal turned and regarded Sam with an eyebrow on the verge of rising.

Sam scuffed a bare foot on the stone floor, "D'no nuffin," he muttered.

"Thanks, Sam. Mind if we borrow the map?" Ascott rolled everything up and headed for the exit. Shoal hesitated for just a moment, and then went after him.

CHAPTER 20

"We have to hurry," Ascott said, leading the way down the steps of the Exco building.

"Why?" Shoal whispered, feeling very aware of the sleeping town around them.

"Because if we don't go now, someone else will find the treasure."

"No one's found the treasure in well over a hundred years. There's no rush." Shoal stood her ground on the white-stone street. "Besides, it's late, I'm really tired, and we will both think better if we tackle this in the morning."

Ascott hesitated, torn between his appetite for adventure and Shoal's impenetrable stubbornness. In the end, of course, he had no choice; she made sense, even when he didn't want her to. Ascott fell into step beside Shoal as she headed home. Only the cats watched them pass. Streaks of quicksilver, tabby, and ginger, fast as a lightning-strike, they flitted like ghosts in the corner of Ascott's eye. The cats exchanged glances from the deeper shadows and then climbed upwards to the highest white cliffs to report to the council.

The Smith house was quiet and dark, and only the sound of gentle snores echoed the crash of distant surf.

Ascott stood in the lounge, feeling a discomfort verging on burglary. He waited while Shoal vanished into some other room of white stone walls until she returned with an armload of blankets and a pillow.

"You should be fine on the couch," she said, laying out the bedding.

"Yeah, great, thanks," Ascott replied in a stage whisper that sounded loud to his ears.

He sat down on the couch, pulling his shoes off and trying not to look at Shoal, who stood watching him from the centre of the room.

"Thank you," she said suddenly.

"What for?" Ascott felt an absurd stab of guilt.

"You have restored my faith in things that I thought were lost."

"You mean the gods?" Ascott felt bad calling them that. Surely there was a rational explanation for what they had seen and spoken to and, well…Gods didn't exist.

"Yes. The ocean is so vast and so wonderful that it couldn't possibly just *be*. Something greater than us has to come from it."

"Well, if you take into account evolution, everything came from the sea originally." Ascott could feel the sands of reason eroding under his feet.

"The gods didn't evolve," Shoal said with a sudden sharpness to her tone.

"Maybe they did." Ascott mentally cast a line out into dark and treacherous waters, reeling in an idea and seeing if it would get a bite. "The woman—"

"The Lady," Shoal corrected.

"The Lady said she was the personification of desire. If enough people believe something strongly enough, maybe that belief can take a physical form?"

"Or maybe people believe in the Lady and the other gods because they are real?" Shoal turned on her heel and walked out of the room.

Ascott lay on the couch and pulled the blanket over his head. The events of the last week—Kalim, the mysterious journal, the lost treasure of Captain Aarrgh—were all laid out in his mind like a deck of playing cards with too many Jokers.

Sleep eluded him in much the same way that answers to the mysteries of the treasure and Tacus did. He could spend a lifetime searching every island of the Archipelago. On every atoll he would find answers to a lot of questions he didn't even know to ask yet. Some answers to the big questions he had right now would be good. Maybe in the morning after Shoal had calmed down and forgiven him for being rational they could go together and find some.

"Stop looking for answers, and focus on finding the questions." The voice was so close to Ascott's ear it sent him scrambling up the back of the couch in a tangled panic.

"Whathafargleflange!?" Ascott's muffled voice babbled under the blanket as he pulled himself free. "Drakeforth?" he managed a moment later.

"Quite," Drakeforth agreed.

"But...I...there was...Oh." Ascott's questions jostled for priority at the front of his mind.

"I come and go as needed. Yes, you have a lot to tell me. But there is plenty of time for that, although just when will remain to be seen. Yes, there was. Quite extraordinary, isn't it? You should take a moment and gather your thoughts." Drakeforth sat back on the coffee table, crossed his legs and folded his arms.

"Drakeforth," Ascott said again.

"Unless you are suffering some kind of short-term memory loss, we did this already," Drakeforth reminded him.

Ascott decided on the most obvious question. "What is going on?"

"Everything," Drakeforth said. "Everything is always going on. Don't hyperventilate—I know you are asking for specifics."

"I am?" Ascott asked, desperately trying to keep his footing in the conversation.

"Yes. You want to know where the treasure is, how gods can exist in an evolving Universe, and how to save your sister from an unfortunate passing."

"I do? I do," Ascott quickly corrected himself.

"Yes." Drakeforth stood up. "Well, now that we have cleared that up, I'd best be off."

"Wait." Ascott struggled out of the blankets and stumbled to his feet. "What do you mean about asking more questions? I've done nothing but ask questions. I'm ready for some answers."

"So, start asking the right questions." Drakeforth said with exaggerated slowness.

"What…? No. Wait. Who…?" Ascott raised a hand in a gesture requesting a moment. After a few thoughtful seconds he said, "Why do you care?"

"Gods are terribly nosey. We can't help ourselves. We just want to get involved, stir things up and blame you lot when things go wrong."

"You're a god." Ascott sat down again on the couch.

"Did I not mention that? I'm sure I mentioned that," Drakeforth regarded him with a frown.

"You did. You also said you were a gilded teapot salesman," Ascott said.

"No, I said I once knew a gelded teapot salesman. Interesting fellow, no interest in basic human attractions. Obsessed with tea."

"You're Arthur. Which makes you the god of what, exactly?" Ascott lassoed his train of thought and reined it in.

"Arthur is the god of the Arthurians. Or at least, I was. I retired."

"And your retirement plans were to walk the earth and get my sister killed?"

Drakeforth's eyes flashed. "Not at all. To walk the earth and do all the fun things I could never do while I was the patron deity of a very successful cult."

"I can save Charlotte," Ascott insisted. "We found a pool on the Island of Saint Amoeba—it has healing properties."

Drakeforth sat on the edge of the small table and leaned forward. He put a hand on Ascott's shoulder and regarded him steadily.

"She, The Lady of the Sea, is the personification of a desire," Drakeforth said.

"Yes, and she can heal Charlotte. Tacus' feathers grew back."

"Desire is a very personal thing. Tacus wanted very much to

have his feathers restored. He desired it beyond anything else."

"Charlotte wants to be well—she must," Ascott declared.

"*Or*, she may have found in the certainty of her death a sense of purpose and a future that fulfils her greatest desire."

"How can being dead fulfil anyone's greatest desire?"

"Charlotte will still exist; her life-force, what some would call a soul, or the sum total of her experiences and thoughts and memories. She is going to abandon her physical form and take on one that is entirely different."

"What in the hyphen are you talking about?" Ascott's face was wracked with confusion and grief.

"Charlotte has decided to have the sum total of her empathic energy transferred into a building's power system, where she will remain complete and eternal, aware in a way—and hyper-aware in others."

Ascott stared for a moment and then shook his head. "Fine. Don't tell me the truth."

"It's precisely because of this reaction that I don't tell you the truth when we first meet," Drakeforth replied.

"Met," Ascott corrected past-tensely.

"That's one way of looking at it."

Ascott steered the conversation back into more familiar waters. "We found a shipwreck and a secret door."

"The *Bilgepuppy*?"

Ascott nodded. "I found the journal of Captain Aarrgh. It had some entries by Dentine Tubule, the ship's surgeon. Old Sam at the Exco told us that Dentine was also the first manager of the Exco."

"Indeed he was,"

"Did you build the secret room in the back of the Exco? The one with the undersea door?"

"Me? No." Drakeforth looked intrigued. "A door to the bottom of the sea? In the Exco?"

"Yes, it was in a secret room, behind a hidden door."

"Most secret rooms are behind hidden doors," Drakeforth said.

"I know, but this was a secret room with a hidden door inside."

"A secret door, behind a secret door? That seems a bit excessive," Drakeforth said.

"I know, so it must mean something, right?"

"What was the first door like on the inside?" Drakeforth asked.

"What?" Ascott frowned.

"The door that led from the Exco side into the secret room. On the inside, what did the door look like?" Drakeforth explained with uncharacteristic patience.

"It, uhh…I don't think I paid much attention," Ascott admitted.

"If it looked like a door, we have a puzzle. If it looked like anything but a door, then we have a simple answer."

"It…looked like a wall, until we moved the Living Oak filing cabinet."

Drakeforth nodded. "And on the inside?"

"Uhh…there were shelves. The back of the door was hidden by shelves."

"And the other door?"

"Well." Ascott strained his memory, "It was a wooden cabinet which opened up a much larger door when we tried to open it."

Drakeforth leaned in, his eyes gleaming in the moonlight. "What did the outside of the second door look like?"

"It looked like a coral reef?" Ascott answered carefully.

"And why are two doors that look nothing like doors important?" Drakeforth asked.

"Someone really didn't want anyone finding the room?" Ascott hazarded.

"Exactly. More importantly, they didn't want anyone to find the room from either side."

"Who didn't?" Ascott asked, troubled that he might be losing the thread of the conversation.

"Another excellent question. I would suggest that Dentine Tubule discovered the room and used it to his advantage. The Living Oak filing cabinet, with the right encouragement, would produce a morphic field of double-e flux that could easily disguise the door behind it as a wall. The secret door in the hidden room suggests that whoever built the room did not want it found by anyone. Including those who might approach it from the outside."

"Fish?" Ascott asked.

"Maybe. Or the likes of Old Noodle-Nose, She, Captain Crab Hands, and even Hee."

"The old gods?" Ascott felt his mind twisting.

"Some of them. Gods are funny things. They change with the people who worship them. Primordial nature spirits become primitive guardians of society and before you know it you have actual powerful entities."

"Is that where Arthur came from? Some proto-physicist wishing he could understand the true nature of the Universe?"

"Arthur came to be by living exactly when he needed to, exactly where he needed to." Drakeforth's expression made it clear he would not be elaborating.

"So why would someone worship all the gods, including you, and hide it all from everyone, including the gods themselves?" Ascott's brain twitched.

"If he had done something so terrible that it could never be forgiven. Yet at the same time he felt so bad about it, he tried to appease everyone. Without drawing attention to himself."

"You are actually suggesting that Dentine Tubule founded some kind of polytheist cult and then kept it secret from everyone, even the gods he was worshipping?" Ascott squeezed the bridge of his nose between a thumb and forefinger.

"Religion makes people do really weird things," Drakeforth said with a shrug.

"He is linked with the treasure, isn't he?" Ascott asked.

"Yes." Drakeforth nodded.

"What is the treasure?"

"It is the most valuable thing imaginable. The greatest gift and the most important. The really cool thing about it is that it is real. It is not some prank, or idea, or even a voucher for a seafood restaurant that expired a century ago. The treasure is something you can see and touch and understand. To find the treasure is to be changed forever by it." Drakeforth managed to sound reverent.

"It drove at least two people mad," Ascott reminded him.

"Change can take many forms. You have map coordinates and a reasonably dodgy sea chart. Try your luck. See if you can find what you are looking for." Drakeforth stood up and brushed the front of his trousers with his hands. "Now, go to sleep."

Ascott opened his mouth to ask further questions and immediately fell asleep.

CHAPTER 21

To no one's surprise the next day dawned clear and bright. The sea sparkled as a light breeze caressed its surface, and the horizon misted with the exhaust of hundreds of commuting whales.

Ascott woke to the sound of things frying. It took a moment for his nose to wake up and join the conversation going on between his ears and brain. Fish for breakfast. No surprises there. Slipping out from under the covers he padded barefoot to the bathroom. He stood on the cool tiles, experiencing a sense of relief, when the bathroom door opened behind him and Shoal came storming in.

"Shoal?" Ascott yelped, almost turning around in surprise.

Without saying a word, she reached over the tub and turned the shower on. Ascott stood frozen in place. From behind him he heard the soft rustle of Shoal peeling her t-shirt off and tossing it on the floor. A warm flush rose up the back of his neck as the shower curtain slid back and then closed again. With his gaze fixed firmly on the small window in front of him, Ascott reached out and pulled the chain on the cistern.

Taking a deep breath, he turned on his heel and marched to the door, every sense screaming that *right there,* on the other side of that flax curtain, a naked woman was washing her hair with what smelled like Coral Rose shampoo.

Ascott left the bathroom and exhaled.

"Morning!" Sandy said, clapping Ascott on the shoulder so he nearly screamed. "You ready for breakfast?" he asked as he passed Ascott and went into the kitchen.

"Ah, sure." Ascott went and took a seat at the low table. He felt a pang of concern for Tacus. The parrot was out there somewhere, probably cursing other island birds and demanding they feed him.

"Hey, honey," Palm greeted him and started loading the table with platters of fried fish, fried bananas, fried milknut flesh and a tall pitcher of island tea.

"Morning, Missus Smith," Ascott said.

"Where's Shoaly?" Sandy asked, coming into the room and taking a seat at the table.

"In the shower…I think," Ascott replied, his blush freshening.

"She's a terror in the mornings. No point in talking to her until she's had a chance to wake up," Palm said.

Ascott was puzzled by that. On the two occasions, both in the last week, when he had been nearby when Shoal woke up, she had seemed quite reasonable.

Shoal appeared, looking fresh and slightly damp. "Morning Mum, Dad, Scotty." She slid her long legs under the table. "Pass the juice."

Sandy passed the tea. "What are you fellas up to today?" he asked.

"Treasure hunting," Shoal said, loading a plate with flaking fish fillets.

"Oh aye?" Palm asked, her raised eyebrow moving from Shoal to Ascott.

"Well, not really treasure hunting," Ascott said hurriedly.

Shoal scowled, "What would you call it then?"

"I—that is…"

"What treasure you looking for?" Sandy asked around a mouthful of fish.

"Captain Aarrgh's treasure," Shoal said, her gaze fixed on Ascott.

"You don't wanna go messing with things like that, aye," Palm said, reaching out to casually pound Sandy on the back as he started to choke.

"You're probably right." Ascott nodded, eyeing Sandy with concern.

"Why not?" Shoal demanded.

"Some things are not meant to be found." Palm stood up and seized Sandy in a bear hug from behind. With a sharp jerk she cleared Sandy's throat and he lay back wheezing, tears dripping down his cheeks.

"Yer mother is right," Sandy gasped. "The Laughing Man wouldn't like it."

Shoal and Palm immediately laughed out loud. Ascott looked at them both in bewilderment.

"Why is that funny?" he asked when the noise died down.

"It's not," Shoal said and drank more tea.

"Why is it not funny?" Ascott asked carefully.

"When Hee is mentioned, it must be in good humour," Palm explained.

"Hee? You mean the Lau—?"

Shoal pressed a hand across Ascott's face to stop him.

"It's safer to say *Hee*."

"Who is Hee?" Ascott asked.

"Hee is the spirit of the islands. The god from which all bounty comes. The one who gives us everything."

"He sounds like the god of the Export Company," Ascott said with a wry smile. The three faces around the table turned and looked at him. No one smiled in return.

"I'm sorry?" he ventured.

Palm nodded. "Exco don't have no gods. It were built to end such nonsense. Mr Tubule, he was never a fan of gods. Laughing or otherwise. They say the Exco was founded as his way of bringing the modern world to the island and banishing the old ones."

"Did you know this?" Ascott asked Shoal.

"Did you listen to half the things your parents told you when you were little?" she replied.

"Dentine Tubule had a real thing for gods," Palm said. "They reckon he refused to believe in 'em and got angry when people went about their business worshipping them."

"What about Arthur?"

Sandy gave a short laugh. "Arthur, eh? Mostly we just smile and nod at Arthur. We've got enough old gods around here to keep happy without fussing with a new fella."

"Ascott believes in Arthur," Shoal said with a cheeky grin.

"I don't," he replied immediately. "I mean, I've met him. So it's less a belief than a verifiable fact."

Those around the table nodded. Ascott was relieved to see no judgement in their expressions.

The meal continued in silence. Afterwards, Ascott and Shoal did the dishes.

"We going out today?" she asked, swirling the water out of the kitchen sink.

"If you like," he replied, hanging up a dish-towel.

"There's something important going on out there. It's been going on for a long time. I think...I think the treasure wants to be found," Shoal said, frowning at the small whirlpool in the drain.

"I don't think a treasure has an opinion either way. Found or not found. It's just stuff."

"We're all just stuff," Shoal replied. "Right now, we're stuff that is walking around and talking and thinking and feeling. When we stop doing that, we just go back to being stuff."

"Well, yes. But." Ascott realised he had no response.

Shoal continued. "My Nana, she always said life came from the sea and to the sea it would return. For generations we have always buried our dead at sea. Given them back to the fish, the crabs, the worms, and everything else that doesn't mind a free feed."

"It makes sense, there's not really a lot of room for a cemetery on the island," Ascott said.

"It's more than that," Shoal gave him a sharp look. "Nana is all around us. She's in the water, the fish, the soil, the sand. She's in the food we eat and the waves. When I miss her, I just have to go for a swim. Then I know she is still with me."

Ascott felt a sharp sliver of grief cut deep inside his chest. When his parents died, what had he done? Had an anxiety attack and fled.

"I don't even know what happened to my parents after their funeral," he said. "Charlotte took care of everything. Now she's dying, and I'm not even there to make arrangements for her."

"She could come here," Shoal suggested. "We could give her a great send-off. We'd throw a big party and then return her to the sea."

"I want to bring her to the island of Saint Amoeba and see if the silver pool can heal her. Though, I'm not sure the sea is Charlotte's thing. She's quite fond of her technology. Take her away from computers and empathic machines and she'd get bored."

"She wouldn't get bored if she was dead. I don't think the dead care about that sort of thing," Shoal mused.

"Drakeforth came to me last night and…among other things… he said that Charlotte could only be healed if she truly desired to keep living."

"That make sense," Shoal said.

"He said I have started asking the right questions."

"It does help in getting the right answers," Shoal offered.

"He also said we have a map, so we should use it."

"Would be a shame not to," Shoal said.

"So, let's go find this treasure. Then I can get home in time to save my sister."

"Fruity," Shoal said.

CHAPTER 22

Shoal spoke kindly to the outboard motor on her new zip-boat and soon it was purring and ready to go. Ascott loaded the boat with a packed lunch, bottles of Java and SCRAM dive gear. The cats of the island were out in force, lined up on each side of the jetty, watching Ascott carrying each load with inscrutable expressions.

"Give them this," Shoal said, handing Ascott a two-day-old fish wrapped in green-leaf.

He winced at the smell. "Will it scare them away?"

"No, but an offering to the cats is a good way to bless any enterprise."

Ascott took the fish and held it as far away from himself as possible. Turning to the cats, he said, "We're going treasure hunting. Please accept this fish in return for a blessing on the success of our venture."

He waited. The cats just stared at him.

"Right, well, thanks. Here's your fish." He tossed the scaled carcass a few feet down the jetty. The cats pounced, moving in a lithe swarm as they fell on the offering.

"You coming or what?" Shoal called up from the boat.

Ascott climbed down and sat in the bow.

"What did the cats say?" she asked as the boat purred away from the jetty and out into the lagoon.

"Nothing?" Ascott looked surprised. "Do they speak?"

Shoal grinned, "Of course not. They're cats. City boy." She rolled her eyes.

Ascott smiled and unrolled the map. It was faded with age and the gaps between the woven slats of dried sea-plant made clear navigation a matter of guess work.

"*Fyne Tuthe Com*," Ascott read aloud. "Do you know what that means?"

"Fin Tooth is a reef," Shoal replied.

"Can we go there?"

"Of course," Shoal replied, twisting the throttle until the engine hummed and the zip-boat bounced over the gentle swell.

They only slowed when the sea ahead broke into foam, the swirling waves breaking enough to show a low ridge of fan-like coral. "Fin Tooth reef," Shoal declared.

Ascott nodded, turning his attention back to the map. He traced the weathered ink. "According to the map, from *Fyne Tuthe Com* the nearest legible coordinates are either seven grid points north-east or two folds of the map due south."

"Let me have a look," Shoal took the map from him. Ascott watched as she peered at it, the tip of her tongue emerging to touch her top lip as she concentrated. "This is silly," she announced a minute later.

"It's a map. It's an exact guide to where we want to go," Ascott replied with a faint sniff in his voice.

"I know it's a map," Shoal snapped. "What I mean is that I've been all over this," Shoal waved at the Aardvark Archipelago that surrounded them, "and never once have I needed a map to tell me where I am." She jabbed at the map with a long finger.

"Well, I need it. The map tells me that Fin Tooth reef is here, so that means that the island over there is...*Sawce Stayn, Please Ignoor*." Ascott fell silent for a moment. "Okay, *that* island over there is *Goode F'r Milkenutes*. Oh I give up," he muttered.

"Milknut Island?" Shoal asked.

"I suppose. Good for Milknuts?"

"I know Milknut Island, it's absolutely covered in milknut palms. They used to put people accused of crimes on that island. If you survived a week without getting your skull crushed by a falling milknut, it meant you were innocent."

"Were a lot of people found innocent?" Ascott asked.

"Depended on the time of year. Nana always said that hurricane season meant a crime spree."

Ascott opened his mouth to say something obvious, then closed it again. Staring at the map, he said, "Here's Fin Tooth reef, here is Milknut Island. See, they're on the map the same way they are on the ocean."

Shoal kept staring out to sea. "How long will it take you to find the right spot on that map, so I can find the right spot in the real world?"

"It could be a while. Some of the numbers are faded. You know the islands, but they have different names. So if we find the right ones, we can head in the right direction."

"You might want to hurry up," Shoal replied. Ascott stood up. Swaying slightly to hold his balance, he peered out to sea.

"Kalim Aari," he said.

"That's his boat," Shoal agreed. She dropped down and twisted the throttle on the engine. Ascott flailed and fell down, landing hard on the dive gear. He pulled himself into a sitting position and looked at the horizon beyond their wake.

Kalim AarI's boat was moving slowly across the horizon. "Maybe they haven't seen us?" Ascott suggested.

"I hope not," Shoal replied. The boat bounced across the swell, sliding around a reef. Ahead, the sea erupted in the spray of a pair of whales surfacing in perfect synchronicity.

"Whales!" Ascott yelped.

"Breeding spot," Shoal said, immediately cutting the engine power. The zip-boat drifted, rocking gently on the swell.

"Why have you stopped?" Ascott went from looking for surfacing whales to scanning the horizon for Kalim's boat.

"The whales are courting. We can't disturb them," Shoal said.

"I'm sure they won't mind. We can be out of their way in a few minutes." Ascott said.

Shoal gave him a patient look. "City boy. Always in a hurry. Always looking at things, but not seeing them. You wanted to come to the Aadvarks to look at the fish. Well, there they are. But now you're only interested in treasure."

"I'm not only interested in treasure!" Ascott snapped back.

"Sure you are. Fish that everyone already knows about. Treasure that everyone knows about but no one cares enough to go looking for. You are so interested in finding things that don't need to be found you forget about the important things!"

"What things?" Ascott stood up in the boat and waved his arms. "There's nothing else out here!"

Shoal stood up, her eyes blazing, "Everything is out here!"

The memory of Drakeforth's warning that *it was bigger than fish* flashed in Ascott's brain and choked his tongue before he could speak.

"What?" Shoal said with an edge sharper than any coral.

"Everything *is* out here. You, the endless cycle of life, and the one chance I have to save Charlotte."

The whales surfaced again, snorting water out of their blowholes, showering the boat in a drenching spray.

Shoal giggled. "Whale snot," she said.

"Shoal," Ascott swallowed hard. "Shoal, I—"

"Fungus!" she shouted, pushing Ascott aside to leap for the engine. Ascott fell back against the rubber pontoon. The dark blue shadow of Kalim Aarl's cruiser was bearing down on them.

"Hang on!" Shoal shouted. She opened the throttle and the zip-boat leaped out of the water. Leaning hard she turned the boat, cutting across the bow of the cruiser and heading for a deeper channel.

"Can we outrun them!?" Ascott yelled.

"Outrun a boat that size in this dinghy? Of course not!" Shoal snarled. "But we can make them work for it."

The zip-boat scraped over an undersea rock and bounced. Ascott flew up and landed hard. Scrambling for the map, he rolled it up and clutched it to his chest.

Kalim's boat turned to avoid the hidden reef. Ascott let out a shout.

"No! Look out! The whales!"

The cruiser cut through the water like a knife. The water erupted as the pair of whales surfaced, directly in the path of the larger craft.

Shoal pushed the zip-boat into a sharp turn. Their path would cross the bow of the cruiser again as she tried to get between them and the whales. Too late—the cruiser's sharp prow struck the whales as they exhaled, the jet of spray turned dark, and pink-stained water rained down.

"No!" Shoal screamed.

The heavy cruiser churned the water, sliding over the stricken whales as it ploughed onwards.

The zip-boat bounced down the side of the cruiser, the red surf breaking over the bow as they headed to the stern.

"Murderers!" Shoal screamed at the gleaming blue sides of the passing boat. The cruiser sailed past, its turning circle much wider than that of the zip-boat.

"Oh no," Ascott said, his hands running through his hair as a massive, black-grey body rolled in the wake of the passing boat.

"They killed them!" Shoal screamed. Her face wet with spray and tears.

"One's okay!" Ascott almost laughed in relief. The second whale surfaced, its great dark eye rolling past them as it scanned the length of its dying mate.

"I'm sorry," Ascott said as the great creature passed within an arm's length of the rocking zip-boat.

The great tail rose and smacked the water. Ascott heard Shoal yell and then the world turned upside down. *This is how the fish see the sky*, he thought. Then he was plunging into a maelstrom of white noise.

CHAPTER 23

The Buli Fish proves its worth as a provider to potential mates by making offerings of regurgitated food. They are the only known fish who court by kissing. Male specimens have been observed consuming vast quantities of smaller fish and then vomiting their stomach contents prematurely when they approach a suitable female. This proves to be quite awkward for the male as females display a range of behaviours in response. Most female Buli Fish observed swim away, though a few are impressed by this overt display and vigorous mating ensues.

Hard, sucking kisses trailed their way across Ascott's chest. He stirred and mumbled Shoal's name. Opening his eyes, he saw a tentacle waving near his face.

"Shoal?" He sat up. A gentle surf washed over his legs. Warm sand baked under his back. Shoal lay face-down beside him.

"Shoal?" Ascott croaked. On the edge of his blurred vision the arms of an octopus were descending under the crystal blue waters. Shoal stirred and lifted her head.

"What?" she muttered.

Ascott sat up. His head swam and pounded like a storm surge on a reef.

"Are you okay?" he asked.

"Fruity," Shoal muttered. "What happened?" She groaned and rolled over, shading her eyes against the bright sun.

"I think the octopus saved us," Ascott said.

"Why in the name of Captain Crab Hands would an octopus do that?" Shoal asked, sitting up and brushing sand off herself.

"Honestly? I think it might have done it so it could have something else to feel smug about."

"Well, that's just great." Shoal stood up and looked around.

"What island is this?" Ascott asked standing next to her.

"I don't know." Shoal turned slowly. The beach was pure white sand, like every other beach in the Aardvarks. The sand gave way to a stand of milknut palms and beyond that, dense jungle. "They all look the same from this angle," she admitted.

"I dropped the map when the whale flipped your boat."

"It wasn't really my boat," Shoal replied.

"I'm sorry I keep ruining everything," Ascott said.

"You haven't ruined anything. That Kalim Aari, he's ruined two whales' lives, burned your house down, destroyed three boats and is a complete bad-word."

"A complete bad-word?" Ascott stared at Shoal.

"Yes. You know what a bad-word is, don't you?"

"Of course." Ascott chuckled. "I've just never heard it put quite like that before."

Shoal's eyes flashed fire. "You're laughing at me."

"No, absolutely not." Ascott swallowed hard. "If I had to be stuck on a deserted island with anyone, I'm glad it's you."

"We're not stuck, city boy. It will be a long swim, but I can do it. We could always make a dug-out, or a raft."

"We should explore," Ascott suggested.

"Good idea. I'll catch some fish and get a fire started," Shoal replied.

Ascott caught himself before he spoke. People here related to time in a different way and very little was ever done with a sense of urgency. He sat down again on the warm sand while Shoal waded into the shallows.

Ascott dozed in the sun. Every part of his body felt warm and content. The topic of his next book, he decided, would be the advantages of an island lifestyle. If everyone knew what this felt like, the world would be a different place. People would abandon the drudgery of cities and spend their days sleeping in the sun.

This was an experience that he needed to document.

The smell of burning sea-plant and driftwood caressed his nostrils. He sat up and turned in that direction. Shoal knelt in the sand, a small fire kindling in front of her.

Ascott made his way towards her. "Hi," he said.

"Hi yourself," she replied, and laid a fish on a stick across the fire.

"Once Charlotte is okay, I'm coming back here to stay," Ascott said.

"Sure you will. You'll go back to your big city and everyone will love your book. They'll be amazed at all the fish you discovered that no one ever knew about before. You'll be too busy being clever to remember us."

"I don't care about the fish," Ascott said, sinking to his knees next to her.

"Of course you do. It's what makes you who you are," Shoal replied. "To you, each and every one is something new and exciting. It makes you kinda weird to be around."

Ascott had no answer to that. They ate fish and watched the sun sink towards the horizon until the sky turned the same colour as the embers.

"Well, if we are going to find the treasure, we need to start making a raft," Shoal said, standing up and dusting the sand off.

Ascott followed her up the sand and into the trees. The jungle seethed with life. It rustled and called. Shrieked and burbled. "It's noisier here than it is in the city," Ascott shouted to be heard above the cacophony.

"It's life," Shoal replied, grinning at him over her shoulder.

They walked along natural pathways that wound through the trees. In places stones formed natural steps and, unlike the wild island of Saint Amoeba, the undergrowth here was almost civilised.

A waterfall dived from a high cliff and plunged into a pool of water as clear as glass. Ascott and Shoal rinsed the last of the sand and salt from themselves under the pounding deluge. Behind the waterfall the rock curved inwards, forming an alcove which grew into a cave the deeper they went.

"The roof is glowing," Shoal whispered. The damp rock shimmered with the thread-like tails of glow worms. They were so thick overhead they reduced the pitch dark to a just-penetrable gloom.

Passing under the star-scape of glowing worm bottoms, Shoal and Ascott reached the far end of the tunnel. The path here was more pronounced, winding down a steep valley through dense, humming jungle.

"The stones are different," Ascott said, barely able to make out Shoal in the dark.

"Different to what?" she replied.

"To the stones on the waterfall side. These ones have been melted by great heat. I didn't know there were volcanoes in the islands."

"What's a volcano?" Shoal asked.

"So that's a no, then. A volcano is a place where the melted rock inside the planet has spilled out on the surface."

Ascott heard Shoal stop a few feet ahead of him. "Really?" her voice floated back.

"Yeah, it happens in lots of places. Imagine a mountain with fire and smoke coming out of the top." Moving forward carefully, Ascott found Shoal by bumping into her.

"I'd like to see a volcano—and horses. I have a few pearls riding on whether they or not those things are real."

They moved on, through the warm gloom of the jungle. "Lights," Shoal said a moment later. "Down there. Maybe it's one of your volcanoes?"

"Maybe." Ascott took the lead and went down the path as it switchbacked down the steep slope.

The trees closed in overhead, forming a tunnel like the waterfall cave, but without the soft light of the glow worms.

"I can't see a banjo thing," Ascott complained as he walked into a tangle of branches.

"Use your feet, city boy, it's like standing on the pitching deck of a boat." Shoal walked past him. "Just follow me."

He did, and more by luck than footwork he reached the bottom of the winding path without tripping up. Ascott was sure the vines were moving in the gloom.

In the rocky basin at the bottom of the path, attempts had been made to clear the jungle. It seemed a futile effort. Stakes decorated with carvings of wood and stone decorated the trees. To Ascott, the carvings looked like women, if the carver had never seen an actual woman and only had a few vague details to work from.

They moved down the path, towards the source of the flickering lights. Burning torches formed a perimeter around a cluster of wooden huts that made up a small village in the cleared centre of what Ascott now believed to be the crater of a dormant volcano.

CHAPTER 24

"What kind of people live at the bottom of the crater of a dormant volcano?" Ascott wondered aloud.

"The same kind of people who wear clothes made of bark and never shave," Shoal replied.

Ascott turned slowly and took in the small crowd forming a circle at the edge of the flickering torchlight.

"Hello," he said.

"I think they're pirates," Shoal whispered. Ascott wanted to laugh, and to say, "There haven't been pirates in these waters in over a hundred years." At least until Kalim Aari arrived, he thought.

The men who were watching them wore old-fashioned clothes and hats, albeit fashioned from leaves and vines. More than one sported an eye patch made from woven flax-grass. Their hair and beards would have put Arthurians to shame—thick and long, some matted and rope like. Others wore their beards braided and sculpted into shapes like octopuses, or trees growing from their chins.

"Do you think they can understand us?" Ascott whispered.

"Eh fella, you speakem lingo?" Shoal said loudly.

A mutter rippled through the crowd. Ascott couldn't make out what they were saying.

"You g' sta'fish in y' lug 'oles aye?" Shoal asked.

The group parted to make way for a man with so much polished wood and stone braided into his beard, he crunched like a gravel path with every step. His grass coat was decorated with stone beads and his hair stood high on his head, wrapped in a towering "do that resembled a beehive.

"G'arn y' holes!" he barked. The others shuffled backwards into the shadows. "Y'n all. Y'kin us. Y' gin' die noo."

"He said we've seen them so they are going to kill us now." Shoal translated.

"What? Why?" Ascott stepped forward, jostling for position with Shoal, who was quite ready to get the fight started right away.

"Listen," Ascott said. "We've come a long way, and been through quite a lot. I'm sorry if we've upset you. But we're not going to just let you kill us for stumbling around in the dark."

"Oo'sidas!" the man in front of him shouted. "Keel 'aul t' sc'bby dogs!"

The night air filled with the sound of weapons of stone and wood being drawn from palm-front belts.

"Aye cap'n," the men chorused.

"Run," Shoal whispered, raising her fists.

"You first," Ascott replied, wishing he had a weapon at hand.

A rainbow of plumage burst out of the darkness. It beat the air with iridescent wings and ruined an otherwise perfect entrance by landing on the towering beehive of the captain's hair and nearly knocking him down.

"Bithcuith!" Tacus squawked.

"G'n ye' dramin bayd!" The captain's hands beat about his head. Tacus flapped his wings and tried to unhook his claws from the captain's hair, which had started to buzz ominously.

"Tacus!" Ascott yelled and darted forward to snatch up the flailing parrot.

A ring of swords, spears and stone clubs levelled around Ascott. He froze, arms outstretched.

"Leave him alone!" Shoal yelled. "Tacus, come here, birdy!"

Tacus snapped his beak at the tiny buzzing things Ascott could see emerging from the depths of the captain's hair. Then the parrot took flight. Flapping his bright wings hard, he made the short hop from the captain's hair to collide with Ascott at chest height.

"Bithcuith!" Tacus squawked.

"Tacus," Ascott stroked the bird's plumage and let him nibble his fingertips.

"Ho' ye ken mae bayd?" the captain demanded.

"This is Tacus, he's my bird. At least he was until we went to the Island of Saint Amoeba and he got his feathers back. Then he flew off." Ascott felt sure he wasn't explaining things very well, but the stone point spears jabbing at him were distracting.

"Tacus 'ere bin firs' mate o' Cap'n Aarrgh sin' e' were an egg," the captain growled.

"Well, he showed up at my place one morning demanding to be fed. I figured the storm the night before had blown him in. I fed him and he decided to stay."

"Day'mn bayd, dun deser'ed 'is pos'. Ang 'im wit' tha' twain." The encircling pirates rumbled their approval at the captain's order.

"You can't hang him, or us!" Ascott shouted. "If it wasn't for Tacus we would have never found out the secret of the island of Saint Amoeba, or the mystery of Dentine Tubule and the Pisces of Fate."

In the sudden silence even the bees buzzing around Captain Aarrgh's head went still.

"W' ye know o' t' Pysces o' Fayte?" The captain leaned in close and regarded Ascott with a cold and calculating eye.

"We know that it is an important treasure. We know that it was discovered by Captain Aarrgh and his crew over a hundred years ago. They stole it from She, the goddess of the sea."

"They took it," Shoal spoke up, "from the secret pool where she watched over it on the Island of Saint Amoeba."

"Their ship was then sunk in a storm," Ascott picked up and carried on. "Dentine Tubule, the ship's doctor, was the only one to survive and he kept a chart of where the treasure was hidden."

The captain gave a grunt and stepped back, his hands resting on his hips. To Ascott's surprise he startled to chuckle. The sniggering spread through the crew until they threw their heads back and laughed and laughed. Weapons slipped from numb fingers as they laughed until tears left tracks in the grime and glistened like dew in their beards. They rolled on the ground, gasping and clutching their ribs, all shrieking with hysterical humour.

Ascott felt a burning sense of humiliation, made worse because he had no idea what was so funny.

"Was it something I said?" he asked Shoal as she grabbed his hand and started to drag him away.

"It's not always about you, city boy. Let's get out of here."

"Why are they laughing?" Ascott asked again as they pushed into the thick jungle. Tacus squawked as a low-hanging branch threatened to sweep him off Ascott's shoulder. With a beat of his wings he vanished into the canopy.

"They are summoning Heeheehee, the Laughing God," Shoal explained.

"Why would they want to do that?"

Shoal stopped long enough to stare into Ascott's face so he could see her incredulous expression. "They are summoning Hee because they want Him to kill us."

"It seems like an over-reaction."

"You can always write a letter of complaint later," Shoal said.

The path they came in on had vanished in the darkness. Shoal blazed a trail through the thick undergrowth and took the ground rising underfoot as an indication they were going in the right direction.

"More lights," Ascott hissed. He and Shoal ducked behind a tree as a moving line of torch beams came stumbling down the switchback trail a few feet away.

"A rescue party?" he whispered to Shoal.

"We don't need rescuing. Besides, no one knows we're lost," Shoal said firmly.

"We can follow the trail they are on and head back to the shore," Ascott suggested.

Stepping out of cover once the group passed, they started picking their way up the steep hill. Five steps later, the sudden beam of a torch pinned them like a bug on a card.

"Mister Pudding, Miss Smith," a familiar voice announced.

"Kalim Aari." Ascott said the name like it was a curse. Shoal simply growled.

"What in Arthur's name are you doing here?" Ascott demanded.

"Well, after we saw your—sorry, my—zip-boat get capsized by that savage fish, I insisted that the crew conduct a search and rescue operation."

"You'd better hope you never fall overboard. Your crew are mud at search and rescue," Shoal snapped.

"We felt sure you were lost. I shed tears. It was a beautiful moment. We did, however, find this," Kalim lifted the rolled-up sea chart into the light. "By a wonderful coincidence, it led us to this very island."

"You killed a whale." Shoal's tone raised the hairs on the back of Ascott's neck.

"Possibly," Kalim shrugged. "The ugly things seem to be everywhere."

"Whoa!" Ascott caught Shoal around the waist as she lunged at Kalim, screaming in fury with her hands clawing at his face.

"Tie them up, her especially," Kalim said over their heads.

The Citronella twins and Kalim's crew appeared to have come prepared for all contingencies. They carried rope, picks, shovels, and machetes.

Shoal and Ascott were bound hand and foot. Each twin lifted their share of the extra burden and the descent began again.

Kalim brought up the rear, pausing only to stuff a clean hand-kerchief in Shoal's snarling mouth.

The sound of laughter guided them to the circle of burning torches. The pirates were sounding a bit strained. Many of them subsided into wheezing giggles, until they made eye contact with each other, and that set them off again. Kalim's gang looked on in confusion.

"All right! I'm Kalim Aari. Descended from Captain Fencer Aarrgh! I'm here to claim my treasure!"

The laughter renewed and Kalim blinked in furious surprise. "What are you laughing at?!" he yelled at the wild crowd.

"They're laughing in the face of death," Ascott said from his position over the shoulder of a Citronella twin.

"What is that supposed to mean?" Kalim asked.

"It means if you don't untie us and we all start running, then this isn't going to end well. Not for any of us."

"Put them down," Kalim ordered. The twins set the two prisoners down with their backs against a tree.

Kalim plucked the gag from Shoal's mouth. "What is he talking about?" he demanded.

"HeeHeeHee," Shoal said.

"Oh for Arthur's sake. Not you as well?"

"HeeHeeHee, the Laughing God. They are summoning him and he is going to destroy us all," Shoal continued.

"Who in the herbarium is the Laughing God?" Kalim asked anyone who was listening.

"That is," Ascott said, craning his neck and peering into the sky.

CHAPTER 25

The trees folded under the crushing step of the giant. The darkness made it hard to tell where he emerged from. HeeHeeHee just seemed suddenly to be there, striding through the jungle, crushing the trees that barely reached his knees.

"You could still make it out of here alive. But only if you run really, really fast," Shoal suggested.

"What…? What is that?" Kalim stumbled back, looking up and up.

"Hee," Shoal said. "The eldest of the gods. The body of a mountain, the mind of a baby."

The pirates stopped laughing and a hush fell over the clearing. With a sigh like a wind tunnel running at maximum, the giant sank to the ground. He folded his legs and blinked slowly at the tiny figures scattered far below.

"He…he's huge." Ascott breathed.

"More real than horses, eh?" Shoal managed to grin.

"I am Kalim Aari!" Kalim yelled up at the massive head. "I am here for my treasure!"

"Ooh…" the hairy pirates chorused.

"I want the treasure that Captain Aarrgh found!" Kalim Aari bellowed.

"HHHHMMMMM…" the giant rumbled, slowly leaning forward until his breath blew across the ground, sending the torches flickering and scattering leaves.

"Give me the treasure of Captain Aarrgh!" Kalim yelled at the brown face as large as the moon. With surprising grace for someone with fingers the size of a whale's tail, HeeHeeHee picked up Kalim by the back of his shirt and lifted him closer to one massive eye.

"Put me down!" Kalim screamed. A rumbling sound like an approaching earthquake sounded deep in the Laughing God's belly. His head fell back and HeeHeeHee laughed at the night sky. The air shook with the vibration of his mirth. The pirates, Ascott and Shoal fell to the ground, pressing themselves into the dirt as that terrible laughter reverberated off the steep walls of the jungle-clad crater. A feeling like he was being shaken apart ripped through Ascott. Opening his eyes, he saw Shoal.

"Laugh!" she screamed.

Ascott started laughing, a shrill scream of merriment that bordered on madness. The physical assault of the god's terrible laughter mercifully faded as he passed out.

"Bithcuiths!" Tacus squawked.

"Innaminute," Ascott mumbled. "Go 'way. Too early."

"Bithcuiths!" Tacus nipped at Ascott's ear.

"Oww!" He sat up, his head pounding and vision swirling. "Tacus!"

"All handth on deck," Tacus crowed.

"Shoal?" Ascott scrambled on his hands and knees to where Shoal lay huddled against a tree. The ropes that had bound them were neatly coiled in a heap nearby.

"Tacus is hungry. There's cookies in the kitchen. Feed him," she mumbled.

"We're not at your place," Ascott said his vision clearing.

Shoal groaned and sat up. "What happened?" she asked.

"Cup of tea?" Drakeforth asked, looming over them with a tray laden with silver teaware and delicate shinzin cups.

"Drakeforth," Ascott gingerly climbed to his feet. "Yes, a cup of tea would be lovely, thanks."

Drakeforth nodded and poured. Even Shoal accepted one of the dainty cups without question.

"Introductions now I think, yes?" Drakeforth said. Stepping

aside, he revealed the gathered pantheon.

The hairy pirates were huddled together, looking warily at the various forms who had gathered at the giant feet of HeeHeeHee.

"She, Goddess of the Sea, I believe you have already met." The features of the silver form swirled into a smile.

"Captain Crab Hands, protector of sailors everywhere." An old salt, so crusted he looked like his beard and hair were frosted with ice, gave them a grim nod and clacked his pincers.

"Old Noodle Nose, who has kindly interrupted his annual nap to attend this occasion." A strange, hunched figure with grey-green skin whose lower face was a mass of swirling tentacles raised a green-skinned hand and waved, while yawning audibly.

"And no gathering of the old gods of these Islands would be complete without Our Lady of The Last Breath."

Looking at her took Ascott's breath away. A ghostly figure, wreathed in dark sea-plants, her face an exquisite, haunting, alien beauty. Our Lady's eyes were dark with sorrow and he knew with a chilling certainty that she was Death.

"And you, Arthur," Ascott said.

"Certainly not. I'm just here to observe. I have retired, you know. This god business is nothing to do with me anymore."

HeeHeeHee made a grizzling noise like an iceberg calving into the sea. She, goddess of the seas, flowed upwards in a towering pillar of water. The giant settled and burbled happily as She fussed over him.

"Now, I suppose you expect to see the treasure of Captain Aarrgh?" Drakeforth asked.

"Sure, we have come this far. I think we have earned it," Shoal said.

"No," Ascott said. Taking Shoal's hand he addressed the gather-ed gods. "The treasure is too much to be understood by anyone. It drives people mad. I could live without that, thanks all the same."

"You're not even curious?" Drakeforth asked.

Ascott shook his head, not trusting his mouth to say the right thing.

"You call yourself a scientist, yet when offered an opportunity to comprehend one of the true wonders of your Universe, you refuse?"

"Insanity would make the rest of my life even more challenging," Ascott said.

"Not half so challenging as going through it not knowing," Drakeforth replied.

Ascott took a step forward, then a step back. He turned to Shoal, who just stared at him. Finally, he sighed and raised his hands in a gesture of defeat. "Fine. Show us this wonder of the Universe."

The gods, except for HeeHeeHee, parted, and Drakeforth led Ascott and Shoal to where the pirates waited in solemn silence.

"Ascott Pudding, Shoal Smith, may I introduce you to Captain Fencer Aarrgh."

The captain stood up, and then bent over in a sweeping bow, "Charm'd t'be shure." He smiled, showing a mouthful of blackened tooth stumps.

"You? You are Captain Fencer Aarrgh? But your ship sank a hundred years ago."

"Aye, "tw'r a tee'ble storm. N'tchure hath no fu'ry like an a'gry goddess an' She w'r mighty p'ssed," Captain Aargh said.

"But Dentine Tubule—his journal?" Ascott asked.

"A scur'y dog!" Captain Aargh snarled. "Sa'ed hisself 'e did. Aban'oned the *Bil'puppy*. Left us to our curs'd fayte."

"You stole the Pisces of Fate. That's the treasure. You stole it from She, then when she sank your ship in a hurricane you managed to come ashore here, and you and your crew have been here ever since?" Ascott's analytical mind stated the obvious as frequently as it asked the questions he didn't have the answers to.

"Aye," the captain nodded.

"Dentine Tubule made it back to Montaban. He set up the Export Company and never went near the ocean ever again," Shoal said.

"W'd ye? If'n e'ry god of sea and shore we're 'n out to get ye?"

"The temple in the secret room. He was praying to all the gods for forgiveness," Shoal said.

"But the Exco was designed to bring the modern world to the

people of Montaban, educating them so they wouldn't worship the old gods anymore, and they would—what? Die?"

"Tubule didn't count on the stubbornness of the islanders. They'd been paying lip service to me since the first missionaries arrived," Drakeforth said. "It would take a lot more than a few books and tourists to make them abandon their culture."

"It's who we are," Shoal said.

"So whose body was in the wreck?" Ascott asked.

"People have been stumbling on the wreck for years," Drakeforth said. "Not all of them managed to talk their way out of the octopus' clutches."

"From the sea we came, and to the sea we return," Shoal said.

"But Captain, how have you lived so long?" Ascott asked.

"Fate be a tricky gam'. If "twere a lass, she'd be fine to spy, but queer in t' head," Captain Aarrgh said.

"Hee!" Drakeforth called up to the brown mountain. "Where's your fishy? Show me the fishy and I'll give you a cookie!"

Shoal stifled a snigger, but Drakeforth's face remained impassive.

The massive head of HeeHeeHee lowered and a hand swept down through the trees. The earth trembled and opened. Shoal and Ascott clung to the nearest tree as fresh water burst up in a wild spray.

When the mist cleared they saw a circular pool, with canals running from it to the points of the compass.

"HEEHEEHEE…" the Laughing God chuckled. "FISHY," he boomed. The water of the pool boiled and a golden shape rose up, gleaming in the last of the night's silver moonlight.

A golden statue of a fish floated on the surface of the pool. Water flowed in a torrent from its open mouth and Ascott blinked.

"It looks just like the one in Dentine's painting." He sounded disappointed.

"Appearances are many things, but fortunately not everything," Drakeforth said. "It's not what it looks like, but what it does—what it is—that is so important."

The gathered gods looked on in reverence as Drakeforth led Ascott and Shoal closer.

"The Pisces of Fate. Unique in the Universe, it holds the heart of a neutron star. Within those most remarkable of all stellar objects, the Universe is made. In your normal, everyday star, elements combine through fusion. Hydrogen becomes helium all the way down to the heavier element of iron. But in a neutron star, things go much further. Atoms combine and reform all the way to gold."

"So, the Pisces of Fate is a machine for making gold?" Shoal wrinkled her nose.

"Not a machine for making gold..." Ascott's mouth dropped open and he sank to his knees at the edge of the pool. "It makes life."

"Water passes through the Pisces of Fate and the simple elements are converted to heavier elements. The water remaining flows out, through the canals and into the sea. Over aeons, the atoms combine to form molecules. Molecules link up to form sugars, proteins, and life takes on its own myriad of particular forms," Drakeforth said.

"Kalim Aari would have done something terrible to it," Ascott managed.

"Probably. For a mysterious object that arrived here when the world was young—forming this impact crater, in fact—it's certainly a delicate piece of sculpture," Drakeforth said.

"We need to put it back, to hide it," Ascott scrambled to his feet. "Make Him put it back."

"HeeHeeHee!" Drakeforth yelled into the blacked out sky. "Time for Fishy to go bye-bye!"

A sigh like a tsunami sliding over a gravel beach came down from on high. The Pisces of Fate subsided into the pool, and the earth closed over both it and the canals that carried the elements of all life out to the primordial nursery of the sea.

The gods departed with the first light of dawn. HeeHeeHee sank into the earth. She flowed away, back to her ocean. Old Noodle Nose and Captain Crab Hands were just...not there anymore. Our Lady blew Drakeforth a cold kiss and faded like mist.

Shoal and Ascott sat in the long grass at the top of the crater's edge and watched the sun rise.

Far below, beyond where the golden sand marked the border between blue sea and verdant green, Captain Aarrgh and his crew were wading out to where Kalim Aarl's abandoned cruiser floated in the lagoon, gleaming in the morning light. Drakeforth stood further along the beach, apparently lost in thought.

"It doesn't seem exactly fair," Ascott said.

"Very little in life is fair," Shoal said.

"There haven't been real pirates in these waters for a hundred years. Now we've just given some of the most dangerous ones a new boat and a fond farewell."

"They did promise they would go and terrorise some other part of the ocean," Shoal said.

"They're going to ruin someone's day, no matter where they end up," Ascott replied.

"They deserve a holiday, after being the guardians of the Pisces of Fate for so long."

"There's so much I still want to know," Ascott said. "Where did it come from? How does it work? Is there still new life evolving in the oceans?"

"Gods know," Shoal said, enjoying the warmth of the morning sun.

"That's the most frustrating part. HeeHeeHee probably does. But Drakeforth reckons he'll be napping for the next millennium at least."

"I'm going to build a house down there, by the beach," Shoal said. "And when you come and visit, you can spend your days asking silly questions."

Ascott was silent for a long moment. "Drakeforth said that now we have found the treasure, we will both be the guardians of the Pisces of Fate. Even if I leave the islands. It's quite a responsibility. Watching over the source of all life."

"In our own way, it is what my people have always done," Shoal said.

"I'll talk to Charlotte. If she wants to be cured, I'll bring her here. Afterwards she can go back to the city. I'll stay and finish my research," Ascott said.

"I don't think you will ever finish asking silly questions."

From the rustling canopy of the jungle a parrot with a fiery rainbow of feathers burst into the sky. Wings outstretched, she caught the warm updrafts as they collided with the cooler air over the ocean. Tacus lifted his head from under his wing and blinked.

"Bithcuith!" he squawked and threw himself skyward, the sun reflecting off his iridescent wings as he soared upwards, joining her in the dance.

UNCERTAINTY OF GOATS

A DRAKEFORTH SHORT STORY

Historically, there has always been conflict between the various sects and factions that evolved from differing interpretations of Arthur's Tellings.

The truth of Arthur's early years is a matter of speculation and conjecture. The New Gruffen Church of Arthur, *which in 896 elected a goat as their spiritual leader, holds the following account sacred. (Unfortunately, Algaenian Probabites—kwho preached a doctrine of Arthur as a model of irreducible probability that could not be represented by a physical form—assassinated the* Capra Pontufex, *thus demonstrating they were not kidding around.)*

This is a record of the early life of Arthur, as the New Gruffen Church believes it to have unfolded 1500 years ago...

As a simple man without education, irony was not a word that Agelast, son of Lalochezia, claimed to understand.

A goat-follower who made balloon animals as a hobby, Agelast's life was by its very nature nomadic. This transitory existence was a necessity of his job, which required him to follow his goat herd and, by happy coincidence, gave him a regular supply of the intestines from which he created his inflated sculptures.

For Agelast, balloon-animal construction was the sweetbread atop the cake of his fulfilling life. He had a wife, children, and the companionship of his fellow goatherds, all of whom wandered the bleak and windswept plains of Eastern Mumpsimus. His people had lived on this harsh and unforgiving land for generations, always trailing in the wake of their herds, eyes downcast to avoid stepping in anything pungent. This need for a watchful eye on the ground meant that Agelast's people had no word for horizon and over three hundred words for goat dung. This cultured ignorance protected Agelast like a goatskin raincoat as he skilfully constructed complex models of goats from their own colons while tiptoeing gracefully through the scattered leavings that marked the grasses' passage through the herd.

Agelast watched with a sense of pride as his children grew from squirming babies into healthy, windswept children who could deftly tiptoe for miles. At night, he would tell his beloved wife, Gowpen, that the future of the family herd was safe with their sons Jumentous and Quidnunc. Their eldest daughter, Nelipot, would soon be of marriageable age. When that fateful day came, she would leave the family herd in exchange for a dowry of many goats and they would not see her again until the clans came together at Festival time. Agelast's other daughter was only eight. Her name was Zenzizen and she was the kidney of her father's eye*.

"What of our youngest son?" Gowpen would ask. "Does he not fill your heart with joy?"

Agelast would frown and mutter, "Arthur." The word, translated from the language of the goat-followers, meant '*Goat dung that you can't get out of the cracks in the sole of your shoe*'. It was not the name that Arthur had been given at birth. *That* name had been forgotten.

Arthur did not follow the traditions of his people. He did not pay attention to the wandering of the flocks. He did not throw stones at the large and feral plains-cats, which lurked in the thin grass, waiting to ambush a passing herd. Worst of all, Arthur smelled of the dung that he stepped in regularly. His eyes were

---

* The herds of wandering goats had centuries ago destroyed any apple trees that may once have existed on the grassy plains.

never on the ground. Instead, Arthur gazed beyond the edge of the herd. He looked at the sky a lot and asked many questions.

Agelast welcomed questions when they were on subjects to which his experience and wisdom could be applied. If Arthur ever asked him about the daily travel speed of a herd of goats, their mating habits, the meaning of their various bleats, or even how to tell the health of the herd based solely on a cursory examination of their dung—Agelast could speak at length.

Arthur did not ask normal questions.

"Father," Arthur asked after he had grown enough to graduate from riding his father's shoulders to walking beside him. "How far away is the end of the world?"

For Agelast, the end of the world was a concept, not a fact. His world ended at the edge of the herd. The grass they cropped each day was the land he owned. Tomorrow, they would move on to a new patch, and he would own that land instead.

"T'other side of the herd," Agelast replied.

"But when I ride on your shoulders I can see beyond the end of the herd. I can see tomorrow's grass."

Seeing tomorrow's grass usually meant someone had been dipping his cup into the fermented goat's milk a little too much. For Agelast's people, tomorrow's grass required imagining things that were not yet real. Therefore, they did not exist.

"Grass you're walking on, that's real," Agelast would explain. "Goats—*mind your step*—they're real. Rest of it's in your head."

Arthur thought on this for a long while, and the silence pleased Agelast.

"What about the goats that we can't see?" Arthur asked.

Agelast did a quick count of his herd. His concept of numbers was purely practical. One goat, two goats, and a variation on *herd of goats*. Without needing specific terms for the numbers, he could take in his flock at a glance and know if any of them were missing.

"They're all there," he said.

"Even when we can't see them?" Arthur asked.

Agelast frowned. It made sense that the goats were real. You saw a goat, or goats, or *goats*. You knew when it was dark that they were there, because of the noises they made and their smell. "You can smell them at night," he said.

"What about the other goats, the ones that aren't in our herd?"

This is where Agelast found Arthur's incessant questioning irritating. Goats were goats. Talking about other goats made no sense.

"There's no other goats," he said as a final ruling on the subject. "Until we see them," he added, the logic of this being inescapable.

"So, we make the goats by seeing them?" Arthur asked, his eyes going wide.

"What?" Agelast knew exactly how goats were made, but traditionally that conversation came later in a boy's life, in a complex and confusing conversation that involved a lot of red-faced mumbling by the father and the use of balloon animals as props.

"Festival," Agelast announced. "That's when we make new goats. Everyone comes together, we give them goats, and they give us goats. They make more goats."

The clans only came together once a year, after the snows on the higher steppes had melted and the fresh growth of grass had stirred the bellies of the goats to bring forth their annual young.

"Will we go to Festival soon?" Arthur asked.

Agelast shrugged. "Probably." The cold days had passed and the land was warming again. The goats would lead them, as they always had.

"Probably," Arthur repeated, his mind collating the wisdom of his father and the uncertainty of goats.

As he grew, Arthur found less satisfaction in his father's answers and relied more on his own thinking instead. Following goats as they mowed the grass didn't require much attention, and he made up games and posed questions to himself that would occupy him for days. He experimented with ideas, challenging himself to find answers to the mysteries that plagued him. *How far away is the end of the world? Why can you not see everything? What happens to things you haven't seen yet?*

The annual clan gathering of Festival presented Arthur with more questions. He observed and considered how the presence of other people and their goats fitted in with his developing view of the Universe.

By the time he was twelve, Arthur spent more time silently following the paths in his own head than he did talking to others.

His mother worried about him, his brothers teased him, and his father just frowned as the boy stepped in *kaprino* (a pellet-like scattering).

"The festival is coming," Gowpen reminded Agelast one evening as they sat together by the embers of a drying fire. Agelast grunted and carefully turned the inflated goat intestines so they would dry evenly.

"I wonder if it might be time to send Arthur away," Gowpen continued.

"He'll only find his way back." Agelast had considered leaving Arthur behind several times over the years. For all his lack of ability to survive as a goat-follower, the boy showed a strange kind of intelligence. "Least he doesn't talk much anymore."

"I-think-he-should-go-to-The-City," Gowpen said in a rush.

Agelast turned and stared at his wife. She looked back at him with an expression of calm stubbornness.

"City's not real," Agelast said at last.

"You've heard the stories at Festival, same as I have. Someone always knows someone who met someone who heard about someone who saw The City once."

"Arthur'd die out there without you to remind him to eat," Agelast said.

"Jumentous and Quidnunc have learnt all you can teach them about goats. They'll want to find wives and start their own herds soon. Do you really want to have Arthur beside you until you're too old to walk?"

When she put it like that, Agelast could see her point.

"I'll talk to him," Gowpen said, and patted her husband's knee.

Arthur found the idea of The City intriguing. He asked quest- ions that his mother could not answer, until Gowpen told him

The City was something he would have to find for himself.

This appealed to Arthur's need for self-discovery and exploration. He sank into silent contemplation until they arrived at the Festival. Then he went among the clans and asked everyone if they knew anyone who had met someone who heard about someone who saw The City once.

After two days of walking among the hundreds of goatskin tents, he found someone.

"My name is Arthur," he announced. "I hear you have knowledge of The City."

A girl, close to his own age, regarded the thin and scruffy boy who stood before her. He had the same dark hair and tanned skin as everyone else she knew. Everyone except her.

"I am Magnesia. It means 'pale as milk'. I was not born to the goat-followers of my clan. I was a grass child."

Arthur stared at the girl. Clearly she hadn't been born among the clans that walked carefully in the wake of the wandering goatherds. Her hair and skin were as white as summer clouds. Being a grass child meant Magnesia was a lost baby, who by simple luck had been found before she died of exposure or hungry plains-cats.

"What do you know of The City?" he asked again.

"Nothing," Magnesia admitted, and Arthur turned to leave.

"Wait," the pale girl called after him. "I know nothing of The City, but I have something that does."

Arthur came back and Magnesia lifted a folded cloth out of her tent. She held it out to him.

"What kind of skin is this?" he asked, marvelling at the softness of the hide.

"I don't think it is made from skin. I think it's woven from hair, like mine."

Arthur's nose wrinkled and he jerked his hand back from the cloth. "That's disgusting," he said.

Magnesia shrugged. People often expressed disgust at her pale skin and grass-yellow hair. Goats could be white, but for people to be that colour was unnatural.

"I think this came from The City. The couple who raised me

said that there were signs of people passing near where they found me. The people had returned to the grass."

"All things come from the grass, and all things shall return to it," Arthur said, reciting the words his father believed.

"Except the things that don't," Magnesia replied.

"Do you believe that there is nothing beyond the grass we see every day?" Arthur asked her.

Magnesia gave him a calculating look unlike anything Arthur had experienced before. Somewhere, deep in his nascent adolescence, interest stirred and he looked at her with a fresh curiosity. After a moment, Magnesia tilted her head and leant forward to catch Arthur's line of sight.

"Hello? Sorry if I'm interrupting. We were talking about The City?"

Arthur blushed. He wasn't used to other people wanting to talk about things that couldn't be seen. "Uhh, yeah. How do you know the hair mat came from The City?"

Magnesia rolled an edge of the rug over and pointed at a faded label. "Can you read?" she asked. "Of course you can't. I had to ask someone who does. It says, *Donut Bleech. Cyty of Errm.*"

"What does that mean?" Arthur whispered.

"I think it means that The City is called Errm. There is a man there called Donut Bleech. He may know who my parents were and why they were travelling across the Eastern Mumpsimus."

"If he knows all that, he must be a very wise man indeed," Arthur agreed. "I would like to meet this Donut Bleech."

Magnesia unfolded the cloth. "See these patterns—they're woven into the fabric. They show where things are. I think this green blob is the plains we live on, and the blue-coloured part is the edge of the world. Which means The City would be this bit here."

Some accounts insist that the journey of Arthur from the Festival of Goats to the city of Errm took forty years. More secular scholars agree the journey could not have taken forty years, and that the word for hours— *mok*—was mistranslated as the word for years—*muk*—in early analysis of the ancient Logorrhean texts, from which much of what we know about Arthur's early years is drawn.

Arthurians today agree that Arthur travelled the short distance on foot in a reasonable amount of time, giving rise to the proverb, *"Arthur does not muk about."*

History (as written by The Victors) tells us that the city of Errm stood on the coast of the Argoan Sea and was crafted from local limestone and marble. The walls and buildings of the city reflected the late afternoon sun with a blinding glare, leading the citizens to proudly say that all who approached the great city did so with their heads bowed.

Beneath the retina-searing facades, Errm had all the common features of an ancient city where thousands of people gathered to live and work without the benefits of such infrastructure details as trash collection and the removal of dead beggars off the street.

When Arthur and Magnesia arrived at The City, they plunged into a river of fast-flowing humanity and animality that flowed into Errm like an open drain into a cesspit.

With its myriad sights and smells, some so strong you could almost see them too, Errm delighted and amazed Arthur. Everywhere people jostled and bounced off each other. They collided and congregated in small groups intent on an unknown purpose, before separating and going off in different directions. To Arthur, so unused to seeing large numbers of people in one place, it seemed that when the groups formed, and then dissipated, there were more people leaving the group than had arrived. He absorbed it all, adapting his nascent views and ideas about the Universe in light of his observations and conclusions.

He pushed (and shoved) onwards to the heart of Errm and joined many other wanderers, and people who could not afford to work full-time as beggars, in the courtyard of the temple of Phrontisterion, Goddess of ideas and scholarly debate.

Here, men and women gathered to discuss and argue matters of philosophy, politics and religion. Occasionally, a wide-eyed lunatic accosted the wise and spoke of a new way of thinking based on evidence, called *scyence.*

The more educated dismissed scyence as a fad much like the short-lived religion of *Degustation,* whose adherents taught that the Universe was nothing more than a banquet of many courses for unseen gods whose dining habits caused the varied fortunes of men. Degustians lived in fear of an apocalyptic event they called *The Cheque,* at which time the world would end as the divine diners fell upon each other in an apocalyptic orgy of violence and arguments over the unanswerable question of *Who Ordered What?*

It is written that Arthur learned a great deal during his time in the city of Errm. He ate at the various street-side food stalls and spent much time in the public *kazitoria facilities,* popular among those who had not yet learned to avoid the wares of the various street-side food stalls.

The wider community of religious zealots in Errm fell into two broad categories. At one end of the spectrum were the *gross prophets.* They engaged in blood sacrifice, did not bathe, and imposed strange dietary restrictions on their followers. The other type were the *net prophets,* who focused on gaining followers, and taking whatever cash and worldly goods they could convince them to part with. It intrigued Arthur that no one found this odd or offensive. Everyone believed in something and used a variety of writings, philosophies, and explanations to justify their belief.

The questioning and heated debates thrilled Arthur. He spent all the hours he could in the courtyard, listening to the men and women speak.

Depending on the calendar consulted, it is written that in the third week of the month of Zot, or the seventh week of the quarter of Curdle, or on the eve of the transit of the Bifurcated Tonsil into the constellation of the Moth, Arthur's First Revelation was made to the people.

The Prophet Able, the self-declared voice of The One True God, had paused in his current sermon to drink some water. This momentary lapse in monologue left the floor open for his audience to interject with questions, comments, and offers of ways to make a massive income in a few minutes a day, working from home.

Arthur, who had thought long and hard during his time walking the courtyard, stood up. "Prophet Able, how do you know that your One True God is *The* One True God?" the boy asked.

The Prophet Able put down his cup and regarded the earnest-faced young man with a narrowed gaze.

"If The OTG was not The OTG, then the sun would not rise in the mornings," he declared with absolute certainty.

Arthur thought for a moment. "That would make sense. But what if the sun rises anyway?"

A murmur went through the crowd. Actual questions instead of the usual mud-flinging were rare at these sermons.

"Of course the sun rises anyway, that is your proof that The OTG is The OTG."

"I don't think that is right." Arthur's voice almost cracked but he held the smouldering ember of an idea in his mind and he blew on it gently while adding some dry cynicism. "The Quagans told me yesterday that the sun is a golden egg laid by the Great Duck, and it cracks open every morning and slides across the skillet of the heavens. What if they are right?"

"Then the egg is laid and cracked and sent on its journey by the will of The One True God," the Prophet Able replied.

"Then...why doesn't the Great Duck tell his followers, who are few in number, but great in spirit, to worship The One True God instead?"

The Prophet Able nodded. He had the perfect answer for this one. "Because the garden of The One True God is only open to those who give their hearts to his glory."

"And what happens to everyone else?"

"They spend eternity treading water in the bottomless cesspit."

"Why?" Arthur asked, genuinely perplexed. "Did they do something wrong?"

"They did not heed the word of The One True God!" the Prophet Able shouted loud enough for the people at the back to hear him.

"What if they did not hear the word of The One True God?" Arthur asked.

"Then they shall live and die in ignorance. Doomed to repeat their lives until they do," the Prophet Able announced, and many in the audience nodded, for it was so.

"That seems a bit unfair. What if they lived somewhere remote and never heard of The One True God? It's hardly their fault that The OTG didn't give them the chance to hear the truth."

"The OTG is everywhere. His voice is in all things and to hear it, one must simply listen."

The crowd nodded at this sound argument, a few juggling hot bare-nuts in their hands to cool them for eating between exchanges.

"If The OTG is everywhere and talking loud enough to be heard, then why do so many people either not hear it, or hear some other God?"

The Prophet Able's grip on his stick grew white-knuckled. "Because they choose not to listen to The Truth."

"But to avoid treading grey-water for all eternity, why not just accept your OTG as The OTG and cover your bets?" Arthur asked.

"Yeah," a hot-bare-nut juggler called from the anonymity of the crowd. "Most of us just go to temples for festivals and don't really pay much attention to the Gods till we need 'em."

"And what does God want with all that money you lot are always asking for?" another devotee called out.

"The donations go towards spreading the teachings of the One True God," Able replied.

"Spreading the teachings? You've not left the square since the year of Black Cheese!" a woman in the audience snapped.

A chorus of angry murmurs rippled across the crowd.

"What's he offering you that The OTG isn't!?" Prophet Able pointed his Stick of Redemption at Arthur.

"He has a point," a bare-nut vendor said through the shimmering heat above his tiny stove.

"Yeah, what's your great revelation?"

The crowd turned and regarded Arthur with suspicion tinged with hope.

"I'm not a prophet. I'm not here to convince you to follow a religion. I'm just seeking answers, like the rest of you."

"Well, you must have some answers—what are they?" the crowd demanded.

"I…" Arthur took a step back as the suddenly hostile audience made ready to throw their hot nuts at him.

"He's a faker! Just like that guy we nutted last week!" the Prophet Able shouted.

"I can't tell you what I know, because I'm really not sure what that is." A salted bare-nut sailed past his ear. "But!" Arthur raised his hands in hasty defence. "I can tell you what I don't know. Which is quite a lot and may help explain what you don't know either."

The crowd paused as they mentally worked through the contortions of the previous sentence.

"You what?" someone shouted.

"He says he knows what he doesn't know," a helpful voice explained.

"How can he know what he doesn't know, because then…he would know it!?"

The crowd fell into a cacophony of loud debates on the paradox of knowing what was unknown.

Arthur tried to slip away unseen and found his way blocked by a wall of confused faces.

"Explain what you mean!" they demanded.

"I can't!"

"Then why did you say anything?"

Arthur opened his mouth and then closed it again. The crowd ebbed into watchful silence.

He tried again. "What if we are just like goats?—No, wait!" Arthur added quickly as the crowd swelled with indignant fury. "A herd of goats looks like one living thing. It moves, eats, poops, has babies, and moves some more. Only when you look closely at a herd, you start seeing the smaller parts that make it up. Lots and lots of goats that from a distance look like one big animal. But they are all different."

"How are people like goats then?" an audience member demanded.

"Each of us is one tiny thing in the middle of a whole lot of other things. But we are all looking for the same thing—just like the goats."

Someone with a different opinion chose that moment to throw a bare-nut at Arthur. He ducked the missile and the crowd's angry murmuring rose again.

Arthur worked on putting ideas that he could hardly comprehend himself, into words that the audience, who were one burning torch away from being a mob, could understand.

"You only know what you see, or feel, or hear, or taste."

"What about smell?" a voice asked.

"Or smell. Those things, what we sense, those things are real. You can never know what someone else perceives. Their reality is unique."

"The word of The One True God is real," the Prophet Able declared.

"For you, yes," Arthur agreed. "But for someone who has never heard of The OTG, it doesn't exist. It's not that they just don't know about it."

"Blasphemy!" the Prophet shouted.

"If ideas were real, then yes, everyone would know about your God. It would be real for all of us. Even if we hadn't heard of it. But the idea doesn't exist for people until you tell them it is real. That's not blasphemy, that's just you needing to get out more and meet new people."

"He's right about that!" the Year of the Black Cheese woman shouted.

"Do you know why goats don't ask questions?" Arthur asked.

"They're dumb?"

"They can't talk?"

"They are in league with the evil cabal who rule us in secret from the shadows?!"

"Goats have all the answers they need," Arthur said. "A goat's entire existence is about eating grass and making more goats. When they eat grass they look far enough ahead to see the next mouthful. Then they walk to that and never give any thought to anything else, because that is all they want."

"That's not people, though," a man queuing for bare-nuts called over his shoulder.

"Maybe it is," Arthur replied. "You come to this square seeking easy answers the same way goats follow grass. As long as you are getting satisfying answers, why ask anything else? Everyone here who's preaching their ideas about the truth has found enough answers they can accept. Now they want you to accept those answers, too."

"The prophets want us to eat grass?" a puzzled voice called from the growing crowd.

"No, that's not what I'm saying," Arthur replied.

"Bovinians eat grass. They say cows are sacred and wear helmets with horns on them," another voice shouted.

"This isn't about grass!" Arthur yelled to be heard over the sudden surge of arguments about the nutritional value of various pastures. "I'm saying, don't accept the answers someone else gives you unless those answers create more questions."

"Why?" the crowd asked.

"Exactly!" Arthur nodded.

"What did he say?" a voice at the back called.

"He said, if they tell you to stay off the grass, you should ask why."

The audience started shouting.

"Maybe it's just been sown?"

"What if it's been raining? The grass could get muddy if everyone started walking across it."

"What about other crops?"

"I grow potatoes, can I walk on them?"

"What if there are no roads?"

"What should we do if we see someone walking on the grass?"

The crowd turned inwards as the multitude offered their own interpretations of the goat-herder's words.

Arthur took the opportunity to slip away unseen.

Present in the crowd that day were conjoined twins and later Arthurian scholars of the Palindrome Order, the Brothers Malayalam. They would go on to write the most widely accepted analysis of the First Revelation of Arthur. In their thesis they argued that the true purpose of the First Revelation was not to provide answers, but to provoke thought.

The Malayalams were renowned among their contemporaries as being notoriously argumentative with each other. We often find that the page on the left differs in argument and conclusion from the page on the right.[†]

"I think I should grow a beard," Arthur declared, when he found Magnesia at a weavers' stall.

"Good luck with that," Magnesia replied, her attention on the soft white cloth draped across the table.

"As a disguise, of course. How long do you think it would take me to grow one?"

"Puberty, I should think."

Arthur glanced over his shoulder for pursuers and wondered if he was far enough from the madding crowd to be safe from their quest for answers.

"I have found Donut Bleech," Magnesia said.

"Good, where is he?"

"Donut Bleech is not a he—it's a dye factory in the Weavers' Eighth. I've been asking around and The Weavers' is a neighbourhood of Errm where the makers of cloth of all kinds live and work. This area of the city used to be the Weavers' Quarter, until in the reign of Administrator Doog, the all-powerful SHAMPOO Guild of Shearers, Harlots, Armourers, Magicians, Piemen, Osteopaths, and Obstetricians fragmented. In the chaos that followed that dark time, new guilds were established and existing shop space was divided up to make room."

---

† A century after the brothers' death, the Palindrome Order was engulfed in the cleansing tide of the Edict of Erasable, which decreed that all thought, once committed to the permanence of parchment, stone, or lavatory door graffiti, loses its essence. Therefore all recorded knowledge must be swept clean to allow the thought to be reincarnated as a new and original idea. It has also been suggested that this was simply an attempt to subvert the then-newly conceived idea of copyright law.

"It seems I left you on your own for longer than I realised," Arthur said, when Magnesia paused to draw breath.

"Well, you insisted on spending your days listening to the weirdoes in the square arguing about the meaning of life."

"That was important," Arthur replied.

"Just because something is important, doesn't make it necessary."

The next day, Arthur and Magnesia visited Donut Bleech's workshop on Tureen Street. The smell of ammonia and wet dog filled the air with a palpable fug that captured their attention the way avalanches capture chalets in alpine valleys.

Steam rose from stone vats where wool and cloth simmered in an alchemical mix of yourea, myrea, and etherea. Attendants in spotless white tunics stirred the brew with long-handled wooden paddles. Arthur had many questions; Magnesia only had one.

"We are looking for Donut Bleech," she said to the nearest worker.

The man nodded and jerked his head to indicate they should follow him. At the top of a set of stairs was an office, a desk, and the man they were searching for.

"Donut Bleech?" Magnesia asked.

"Not quite," the man replied. He had Magnesia's pale hair and complexion, and a moustache so milk-white it made Arthur want to hand him a napkin.

"We are looking for Donut Bleech," Magnesia insisted.

"Donut Bleech was the name my grandfather was known by. It's a bit embarrassing, really, but it's what they called my father, and now me."

"We have this cloth with your name on it," Arthur said.

The man gestured them forward and took the folded fabric Arthur held out.

With a practised flick of the wrist, Donut unfurled the cloth and spread it over his desk.

"Well," he said after examining it closely. "This is a Donut Bleech towel."

"I was wrapped in it as a baby," Magnesia explained. "I'm trying to find out where my parents came from. We believe the cloth has clues woven into it."

"This," Donut replied with a calm certainty, "is a commemorative towel from the reign of Administrator Doog. In the dark times after he broke the SHAMPOO Guild's monopoly on most services, many people left Errm. Some of them in a hurry. This towel shows the City, here." Donut indicated a woven patch of colour. "The plains of Eastern Mumpsimus," he waved his hand over the unmarked expanse around the edge of the towel, and then gestured to the space beyond the cloth.

"The plains are that big?" Arthur asked.

"I have no idea. No one who goes there has ever drawn a map. It's enough to know that the grass goes on for a long way and the land is filled with goats and monsters."

"What kind of monsters?" Arthur asked, disappointed that in his years of following his family's herd, he had never seen any real monsters.

"The kind that eats people who ask unanswerable questions," Donut replied with a certainty of ignorance that reminded Arthur of his father.

"Can you tell us who owned it?" Magnesia asked.

"The towel? Probably not. I mean, if it was a monogrammed handkerchief, then certainly."

"Whatsa hangerchief?" Arthur asked, the fumes of the factory making his nose stuffy.

"If you can't help us, who can?" Magnesia insisted.

"Try the gods," Donut suggested.

"Any gods in particular?" Arthur looked up from wiping his nose on his sleeve.

"Take your pick," Donut replied.

"Well…" Arthur thought for a moment and then started ticking candidates off his fingers. "There's Queezycocktail, god of hangovers. His followers preach a philosophy of hedonism by night and silent contemplation by day. Or Varicose, goddess of roads and map-makers. Polysisticos, goddess of fertility, Al'Buhmin, god of omelettes…"

Arthur continued while Donut ushered them out to the street. "A Wizeman once said, there are as many deities in this city as there are fools who believe in them."

"Which wise man said that?" Arthur asked with great interest.

"Tobias, I think. Tobias Wizeman. Good bye." Donut closed the door on the pair and they waited for the steam to clear so they could see where they were walking.

Magnesia frowned. "I think he was hiding something."

"In there? He could be hiding almost anything." Arthur turned and looked at the squat building that appeared to have been built over an active geyser field.

"You didn't notice it, did you?" Magnesia glared in a way that made Arthur feel nervous.

"Yes?" he hazarded.

"The white hair, the pale skin? He looks like me."

Arthur nodded. "Oh, oh yes, I noticed that."

Magnesia snorted, and lifted the hem of her dress as she strode away through the wafting steam.

Arthur hurried after the girl and caught up with her outside a decrepit-looking shop front.

"We don't know that you are related," Arthur said.

"I wonder if he didn't want to admit that he knows who I am?" Magnesia replied.

"Why would he not want mention that? Do you think it is a cultural thing? Like, it would be rude to admit to knowing you?"

"I think he doesn't want us to know that he knows me."

"Or, maybe, he doesn't know you?" Arthur said, a deep frown creasing his brow.

"I'd like to keep an eye on him. We need somewhere we can watch the factory." Magnesia looked around and then marched towards a nearby store. Arthur followed her to see what would happen next.

Magnesia pushed open a door and the odour of fresh paint wafted into the street.

"I'm sorry," a woman called from inside, "we aren't open yet."

"That's fine, we aren't here to buy anything," Magnesia called back.

Arthur stepped inside the store and looked around. Inside the doorway he passed under an archway with a strange, feathered ceiling. It took him a moment to see the legs, but they reached all the way to the ground on either side of the doorway.

Turning and backing up, craning his neck to see the full scale of the bird, Arthur gave an impressed whistle.

"*That* is the biggest thing I have ever seen. When I say biggest thing, I mean biggest of this kind of thing. I have seen other things that were much larger, but they were more similar in size to other similar things."

"We would like to wait here until a man from next door leaves his business premises," Magnesia explained.

"Why? Does he owe you money?" A girl, older than Magnesia and Arthur but younger than some of the fillets sold in the local fish market, appeared from behind a bench. She had red hair, unlike anything either of them had seen before. Tufts of it stuck out in haphazard ponytails through gaps in the leather helmet she wore. Attached to the leather helmet with a complex wire scaffolding were dozens of spectacle lenses of varying shapes, colours, and thickness. It gave her the appearance of a spider in dire need of trifocals.

"Yes…?" Magnesia suggested.

"This is…really big!" Arthur continued. He moved some boxes aside and tried to look at the bird from a different angle.

"It's not for sale yet!" the girl called out, and turned her attention back to Magnesia. "You can't stay here. I'm not ready yet."

"What is this thing? Does it have a name? Did you make it? Are there others?"

"It's an Emperor Pengpong. I never asked. No. I believe so," the girl replied without diverting her frown from Magnesia.

"I love it!" Arthur declared.

"Would you be insulted if I said your friend was weird?" the red-headed girl asked Magnesia.

"Of course not. He is weird. Do you know Donut Bleech?"

"Yes, he owns the factory next door. They make cloth of different colours. Quite the alchemical process. It seems to involve a lot of steam, though. I tell you, some days I go to the market, come back with a nice selection of fresh beans and coully and by the time I've got inside, my vegetables are cooked."

"I think he is up to no good," Magnesia declared.

"Hardly, he's just excited from seeing his first giant Pengpong." The girl waved Magnesia's suspicions away.

"Not Arthur, Donut Bleech," Magnesia replied.

"Oh. Well, I wouldn't know. I'm trying to run a business here. Or at least, I'm trying to try and run a business here."

"Tell me everything!" Arthur blurted, as he approached the counter.

"Start with your name," Magnesia suggested.

"Leisurely Carpool," the girl said, and executed an extravagant bow.

"Magnesia, and that is Arthur," Magnesia completed the introductions.

"What is this place?" Arthur asked.

"This," Leisurely replied with a definite tone of pride, "is my shop. Here I will sell all manner of innovative and exciting curiosities, puzzles, and indoor sporting equipment."

"Indoor sporting equipment?" Magnesia raised an eyebrow.

"Indeed," Leisurely said with the over-active enthusiasm of the true self-believer.

"Aren't sports normally done outside? With balls, clubs and salted fish?" Magnesia hadn't paid much attention to the few organised events they had seen since they arrived in Errm.

"Yes!" Leisurely beamed. "But what about those days when you are stuck inside? No room for club-ball or sissy-fish, someone could get hurt, even if you play by Quentinbury rules. My solution is to develop alternative sports. Ones that can be played indoors, by teams of two to four players. With minimal space required and no need for animal sacrifice."

"How does the Emperor Pengpong fit into your plans?" Arthur asked, his mind returning to the current object of his fascination.

"My Grandfather was an explorer. The Cubits imprisoned him for blasphemy when he refused to accept that the world is a square with six sides. He travelled to places no one else has ever seen and brought things back. One of the things he brought back was this large bird. Granddad said that they grow to over eight feet tall. But that isn't the most interesting thing."

"It isn't?" Arthur asked, his eyes wide.

"Gramps called them Emperor Pengpongs," Leisurely continued.

"No doubt because of their stately poise and majestic countenance," Arthur nodded.

"Because they have no knees and cannot kneel," Leisurely corrected him. "The really interesting thing is their eggs."

"Their eggs?" Magnesia looked sceptical.

"They're surprisingly small for such a large bird," Leisurely explained. She rummaged under the counter and came back with a small box stuffed with straw. "These are Pengpong eggs."

In the box was a pile of small white spheres. Leisurely picked one up and grinned at her audience. "If you are eight feet tall, don't have knees, and you reproduce by laying eggs—"

"You become extinct pretty quickly?" Magnesia suggested.

"Or you lay eggs which do this." Leisurely dropped the egg on the countertop. It bounced off the wood, headed towards the ceiling and, as Arthur and Magnesia watched, rebounded several more times until Leisurely caught it. She presented the undamaged egg to them with a grin.

"I have this idea for an indoor version of Club-ball in miniature. It will have a smaller net, and instead of a stone pit half a mile across, maybe a table which can be used for other things between games."

"Like animal sacrifice?" Magnesia asked.

"Sure, why not?"

"What about the clubs?" Arthur asked, picking up one of the balls before tossing it in the air and catching it again.

"Well, they would need to be smaller too. Ratio is important," Leisurely said, and ducked under the counter again.

"We should probably find somewhere else to watch Donut Bleech," Magnesia said.

"Hang on, this is interesting," Arthur said, missing Magnesia's narrowed gaze.

"I made these," Leisurely said, popping up again. She held up two flat wooden paddles. They were missing the three-inch iron spikes Arthur had seen on regular club-ball bats, and actually looked like they could be wielded by a normal person.

"I must try this!" Arthur blurted, and Leisurely grinned at his enthusiasm.

"Right! You go there, I'll hit the egg to you and you try and hit it back." Leisurely adjusted the prism on her head and dropped the Pengpong egg towards the counter. Before it landed, she swiped at it with the flat paddle. It flew towards Arthur, he flailed with this paddle, and with a soft *punk!* the ball bounced off the flat side and sailed over Leisurely's head.

Arthur whooped in delight. "I win!"

"Well, I haven't decided on all the rules yet," Leisurely said with a slight huff in her voice.

"We really should be going," Magnesia said.

"If you like," Leisurely replied, gathering up the egg from where it had landed on the floor.

"Where are we going exactly?" Arthur asked.

"Somewhere else," Magnesia said in a firm tone.

"We were supposed to be keeping an eye on Donut Bleech," Arthur said.

"Really?" Leisurely returned to an upright position. "What do you want with him?"

"I think he knows something about who I am," Magnesia said.

"Oh…" Leisurely blinked and considered her next words carefully. "You mean, other than that you being a direct blood relative?"

"What makes you say that?" Magnesia asked.

"Oh, I don't know, the white-blonde hair, the pale skin, the cold stare."

Arthur popped up from behind a stack of wooden crates. "She might be right," he said.

"Donut Bleech is gaunt, and pale, and smells like goat's water," Magnesia clarified.

"Well, yes." Leisurely adjusted her spectacles at random.

"Leisurely is correct," Arthur said, returning to the counter.

"It's not just that you have the same nose. You and Donut are the only two people I have ever met who have white hair and skin the colour of milk."

"I keep out of the sun," Magnesia replied tersely.

Arthur nodded sympathetically. "I don't suppose you've met a Spelunker? No? Religious types. Believe that the sun is their God's baleful eye staring down at them. So they live underground. Odd people. Only come out at night so, unlike you, they *really* stay out of the sun."

"What's your point?" Magnesia challenged.

"They are as grey as a dead man's tongue. You've got more of a natural whiteness to you. If you were pale cos you never went out in the daylight, you'd look like a Spelunker."

"Why are you making this about me?" Magnesia said through gritted teeth.

Arthur thought for a moment, and then said, "Because family is important. You wanted to find your family. Your real family. Now we may have. Donut Bleech could be a relative of yours. We just need to find out what kind."

"Even if we are related, I don't have to like him," Magnesia replied.

"You hardly know the man," Arthur said. "He might be quite nice."

"Sunsets are *quite nice*. People are usually not," Magnesia replied.

"There's only one way to be sure. We have to talk to him and determine the truth," Arthur said.

Magnesia turned on her heel and marched towards Leisurely's shop door. "Come on, then," she said without looking back.

Arthur followed her out into the street. The sun was setting now, and it did look quite nice, with the smoke and steam from the various shops and factories making clouds in the sky.

They stepped into the warm, wet interior of Donut Bleech's business premises. Arthur had the unpleasant feeling that this was what walking around the inside of someone else's mouth would feel like.

"Donut Bleech?" Magnesia called over the hiss and clank of steam and press.

"What do you want?" Donut's voice came through the fog.

"Answers," Magnesia replied, and Arthur nodded. He was after all a fan of answers, and the questions they brought with them.

"Answers depend on the questions you ask," Donut's voice replied. Arthur nodded approvingly; that was one of the most profound things he had heard all day.

Magnesia set her hands on her hips. "Very well. My first question is, are we somehow related?"

Silence came in response. At least as near to silence as you can get in a large building filled with the slow bubble of cloth being boiled white.

"Do you need me to repeat the question?" Magnesia asked.

"No." Donut Bleech appeared through the mist. It camouflaged him perfectly, being the same white as his hair, skin and clothes. "Come up to the office, I have something to show you."

Arthur and Magnesia followed Donut past the vats and pipes. They climbed the stairs and entered the warm, and somewhat drier, office.

"What did you say your name was?" Donut asked.

"Magnesia," Magnesia replied.

"If you are who I think you are, then I have never met you before," Donut Bleech said. "You weren't quite born when things went polyhedral in the city. Your mother and father were cloth makers. Weavers of some skill and high regard in the city. Your mother probably made that towel you're carrying. During the reign of Administrator Doog, souvenirs were made illegal."

"So my parents were rebels?" Magnesia looked intrigued.

"Not quite. They were my aunt and uncle. They packed up and left when it became clear that with the breakup of the SHAMPOO guild monopoly, things were going to get hairy around here."

"We think they may have died on the plains of the Eastern Mumpsimus. I was found and raised by goat herders," Magnesia said.

"Sorry to hear that." Donut Bleech waved a hand dismissively. "Anyway, my father, your mother's brother, took over the family business and a couple of years ago he lost his way in the fog and fell into a dye vat."

"He died in a dye vat?" Arthur asked.

"He died as he had lived," Donut Bleech said. "In Swansong Blue and Passing Yellow."

"I'm not sure I want to be related to you," Magnesia announced.

"An hour ago we weren't related. We still might not be. You can go away and we can never speak of this again if you like." Donut's expression suggested that this outcome would suit him.

"An hour ago you weren't related..." Arthur repeated.

"If you walk away now, I can honestly say that I don't know where you are," Donut continued.

"If we walk...he will know our speed, but not our position..." Arthur agreed.

"Does he always repeat everything he hears?" Donut asked with a frown.

"Probably. I don't know. He hasn't done it before."

"Probably...yes...probably..." Arthur turned and, like a sleep-walker, shuffled to the office door and opened it before sprinting down the stairs and out of the factory.

Donut watched him flee. "To be honest, I've worked hard to keep things going here. I'm doing quite well in the family business. But it is *my* family business, not yours. You can't just walk in here and start laying claim to things."

"I wasn't thinking of making any claim. I just wanted to know who I am. Where I come from."

"Well, now you know. Anything else I can help you with?"

Magnesia shook her head. "I don't think I will see you again, Mister Bleech. It's nice to know that I have family, without actually having family."

Donut stared at the pale girl for a long moment. "There is one other thing." He rummaged in his desk and pulled out a small folded cloth. "This embroidery came to me six months ago."

Donut carefully opened the small piece of fabric on the desk.

"The words stitched into the fabric say, '*Gustania Inflate This Domicile*'."

"What does that mean?" Magnesia asked, peering at the fine stitching.

"I have no idea. But I recognise that needlework. It's your mother's. See how she curves her kwits? It's her signature stitch."

"She could have made this any time," Magnesia said.

"Right here, it has a date stitched into it. *The Fourth Tick of Octopus*. According to the Cephalpodium, that was three years ago.

"So my mother is still alive?" Magnesia blinked in astonishment.

"It would appear so."

"Well, goodbye, then." Magnesia extended a hand as Donut opened his arms for a hug. They waved their arms awkwardly for a moment before stepping back.

"Yes. Goodbye," Donut agreed.

Magnesia walked slowly out of the factory and looked around. Arthur was crouched on the street, drawing in the mud with a stick.

"Arthur?"

"It all makes sense," Arthur said without looking up. "Reality, the nature of all things. You and Donut."

"Donut?" Magnesia folded her arms.

"Yes! You see, things don't exist until we see them. Or know them. Or think them. Tomorrow's grass is *probably* over the horizon. We don't know what we don't know, but we know we can have an idea of it. But we can still be uncertain. You wanted to know if the towel would lead you to the mystery of your parents. We couldn't be certain until you and Donut met and both agreed that you were related. Before then, you weren't!"

"Right…" Magnesia frowned "This theory about relatives could use some work."

"Which is the best part," Arthur continued with a gleeful determination. "I don't know anything anymore. Nothing is real unless we perceive it. Everything is just *probably* real. When we left, Donut knew how fast we were going, because he saw us walk, but he can't know where we are."

"We could send him a letter," Magnesia suggested.

"Yes, but that will only mean he will know where we were when we sent the letter. As we keep moving, he won't know where we are from the time he knew where we were."

"Why would we need to keep moving?" Magnesia asked.

"I may have accidentally made some people think for themselves. There was a mob forming when I left the courtyard outside the temple earlier."

"A mob?"

"A crowd of people who wanted to ask me questions about what I don't know."

"You seem quite excited by your ignorance."

"I need time to work this out. Maybe write some of this down."

"How will that help?"

Arthur beamed at her. "I have no idea."

"My parents, at least my mother, might still be alive. I'm wondering if I should try and find her."

"If you like." Arthur added a circle to the complex diagram in the mud.

"I could ask her why they left me in the grass," Magnesia added.

"Yes, yes you could."

"Though… If I didn't look for her, I wouldn't know."

"That is true. Can you step back a bit, please, this is going to need some more space."

Magnesia took a few steps down the street and then slowly turned around. "However, if I did find her and she was dead, then I wouldn't get any answers anyway."

"You would know that she was dead," Arthur suggested.

"Knowing she was dead wouldn't change her being dead," Magnesia replied.

Arthur stopped and straightened up. Magnesia stopped pacing and they turned to stare at each other.

"Except, based on what you're saying, as long as I don't know for sure—"

"She is neither dead, nor alive," Arthur finished.

"I wonder if she would be happier being—what? Probably alive?"

Arthur looked grave. "If you think about it, you knowing for certain your mother was dead, would be what actually killed her."

Magnesia frowned. "As long as I don't know for sure, then she is neither alive nor dead. But what about all those people who do know. The ones who see her every day, or went to her funeral?"

"Irrelevant." Arthur waved his hand. "The only thing that is real is what you perceive and I'm not entirely sure about that yet."

"Oh…" Magnesia's eyes pulsed as she tried to comprehend the concept.

"I need to write this down. A diagram in a muddy street will only last as long as we keep observing it."

"I have an idea." Magnesia shifted her focus to practical matters and vanished into the fog bank outside the dye factory.

She returned a few minutes later, carrying a large white sheet.

"Take this corner and this corner," Magnesia instructed.

She took the other end and they stretched the fabric out over the diagram. "Now, carefully lay it down on the mud."

They lowered the cloth until it lay in the mud across the complicated lines and circles of Arthur's image.

"Okay, lift it straight up, don't let it flap." Magnesia and Arthur rose to their feet. The diagram showed on the sheet in perfect mud-stained detail.‡

"Once it dries, you should be able to take the picture with you anywhere," Magnesia said.

"It's going to need words to explain it all," Arthur said, chewing his lip.

Magnesia nodded. "We'll have to get another sheet."

"Donut Bleech puts colour on cloth, right?" Arthur said, still

‡ Protected by the Knotstick Church of Arthur for hundreds of years, debate over the authenticity of the 'Shroud of Tureen' continues. Modern scientific analysis has proven inconclusive in determining the age of the cloth and the source of the mud stains that the Men of the Cloth claim are on it.

holding the damp cloth in the evening air.

"I think so. They seem to be able to make any number of colours from a few basic ones."

"What if instead of dying a whole sheet, we just asked him to put word-marks on it?"

"Isn't that what the embroiderers do?"

"Yes, but they only make one or two sheets and it takes too long. I'm thinking about making exact copies of the same words and putting them on lots of sheets."

Magnesia turned to regard the mud-stained cloth. "You want Donut to put your picture and your words on lots of bed linen?

"Can you imagine, people going to bed and reading my ideas?"

"I think some people do other things when they go to bed," Magnesia said carefully.

"You mean, sleep? They can do that afterwards."

"Sure, let's say that's what I meant."

"This is going to take a lot of bedding," Arthur mused.

"Why does it have to be so big? Why not make the sheets smaller. Get an embroiderer to stitch them together along one side so they don't get lost or out of order. Then you can put all your ideas on a bunch of sheets that people can take with them without needing some kind of pack animal to carry it."

"An excellent idea." Arthur grinned enthusiastically. "Except, I don't know how to read or write."

"Maybe you can learn? Or, if that's not how it works, we can ask someone to make the marks that mean what you say."

Arthur flapped the sheet. "Then they can tell other people what the marks mean."

"As long as they tell the people that can't read what the marks really mean, and don't make something up." Magnesia frowned at the possibility.

Such distortion of truth was beyond Arthur's comprehension. "Why would anyone do that? If they have their own ideas, they can make their own sheets."

Magnesia nodded. "And because what is on the sheets is true, no one needs to change it. They just have to say it."

They walked down Tureen Street in the rising dusk, the sheet stretched out between them.

"Accuracy will be important," Magnesia said. "We don't want people to misinterpret anything you say."

"I wouldn't worry about it," Arthur said. "I'm not sure anyone will be that interested anyway."